AN OCEAN OF LOVE

Mrs. Winston, sensing that she had overstepped the mark in such grand company, knew enough to play along.

"Madelina will always find me out," she explained with an uneasy giggle. "I try any little trick to get her to eat. She's just too thin for my liking."

"Not for mine!" came in the Duke at once. "She's just perfect as she is. Eh, de Burge?"

"Indeed," was all he could say, his voice cold.

"She'll be the belle of the ball," mused the Duke. "Won't be a female there to match her. Begad, the Earl's daughter herself will have a run for her money, eh?"

"Lady Kitty would think it beyond her dignity to have to run for anything," pointed out de Burge.

It might have been a mild criticism of Lady Kitty, but Madelina did not think so. He was now defending her because he cared for her, there was no doubt about it. No doubt he was as ambitious to marry into a titled family as her own stepmother.

How could she ever have thought that he might be attracted to her, a rich but untitled and unsophisticated girl from a small town on the East Coast of America?

De Burge was ambitious and greedy and loathsome, just loathsome! But, even as she said the words to herself, her heart rebelled, as her lips felt again that soft brush of his lips and her ribs felt the imprint of his strong hand.

And she sensed that she was lost.

Lost to love, in a way that she had never dreamed of and she would never have wished for!

THE BARBARA CARTLAND PINK COLLECTION

Titles in this series

AN OCEAN OF LOVE

BARBARA CARTLAND

Barbaracartland.com Ltd

THE BARBARA CARTLAND PINK COLLECTION

Dame Barbara Cartland is still regarded as the most prolific bestselling author in the history of the world.

In her lifetime she was frequently in the Guinness Book of Records for writing more books than any other living author.

Her most amazing literary feat was to double her output from 10 books a year to over 20 books a year when she was 77 to meet the huge demand.

She went on writing continuously at this rate for 20 years and wrote her very last book at the age of 97, thus completing an incredible 400 books between the ages of 77 and 97.

Her publishers finally could not keep up with this phenomenal output, so at her death in 2000 she left behind an amazing 160 unpublished manuscripts, something that no other author has ever achieved.

Barbara's son, Ian McCorquodale, together with his daughter Iona, felt that it was their sacred duty to publish all these titles for Barbara's millions of admirers all over the world who so love her wonderful romances.

So in 2004 they started publishing the 160 brand new Barbara Cartlands as *The Barbara Cartland Pink Collection*, as Barbara's favourite colour was always pink – and yet more pink!

The Barbara Cartland Pink Collection is published monthly exclusively by Barbaracartland.com and the books are numbered in sequence from 1 to 160.

Enjoy receiving a brand new Barbara Cartland book each month by taking out an annual subscription to the Pink Collection, or purchase the books individually.

The Pink Collection is available from the Barbara Cartland website www.barbaracartland.com via mail order and through all good bookshops.

In addition Ian and Iona are proud to announce that The Barbara Cartland Pink Collection is now available in ebook format as from Valentine's Day 2011.

For more information, please contact us at:

Barbaracartland.com Ltd.
Camfield Place
Hatfield
Hertfordshire AL9 6JE
United Kingdom

Telephone: +44 (0)1707 642629
Fax: +44 (0)1707 663041
Email: info@barbaracartland.com

THE LATE DAME BARBARA CARTLAND

Barbara Cartland who sadly died in May 2000 at the age of nearly 99 was the world's most famous romantic novelist who wrote 723 books in her lifetime with worldwide sales of over 1 billion copies and her books were translated into 36 different languages.

As well as romantic novels, she wrote historical biographies, 6 autobiographies, theatrical plays, books of advice on life, love, vitamins and cookery. She also found time to be a political speaker and television and radio personality.

She wrote her first book at the age of 21 and this was called *Jigsaw*. It became an immediate bestseller and sold 100,000 copies in hardback and was translated into 6 different languages. She wrote continuously throughout her life, writing bestsellers for an astonishing 76 years. Her books have always been immensely popular in the United States, where in 1976 her current books were at numbers 1 & 2 in the B. Dalton bestsellers list, a feat never achieved before or since by any author.

Barbara Cartland became a legend in her own lifetime and will be best remembered for her wonderful romantic novels, so loved by her millions of readers throughout the world.

Her books will always be treasured for their moral message, her pure and innocent heroines, her good looking and dashing heroes and above all her belief that the power of love is more important than anything else in everyone's life.

"Despite the world's seemingly endless wars, strife and turmoil we read about daily in the media, hope still springs eternal in the human breast. And where there is hope, there is love."

Barbara Cartland

CHAPTER ONE
1886

On a balmy late summer evening a carriage drew up outside *The Langham Hotel* in Regent Street.

The doorman then hurried to help out a large eager-looking lady of a distinctly powdered middle-age.

"Oh, my," this lady gushed over her shoulder to an invisible companion still within the carriage.

"You will just *love* this!"

The doorman gave a slight wrinkle of his nose at the lady's very pronounced accent.

American! And no doubt her companion would be another one of those young things who sailed across the ocean to hook a very large prize. An English Duke or Earl!

Sure enough a delicate foot in a purple bootie was extended from within, followed by a small gloved hand.

The doorman seized the offered hand to guide the passenger out and almost whistled.

This one was a real beauty, no doubt about it!

Her complexion glowed and her lips were as red as cherries. Her long chestnut hair framed a face of perfect proportions. And her eyes!

He supposed that their colour could well be called amber, although gold sparkled in their depths.

The older woman gave out a kind of cluck like an angry hen and the doorman was recalled to his duties. He signalled to a bellboy, who flew to collect the luggage.

The older woman sailed up *The Langham* steps, followed by the young girl, whose eyes were widening all the time at the sheer size and luxury of the London hotel.

Why, there was nothing like this back in Albany.

In the foyer the Hotel Manager stood waiting for Mrs. Winston with a smile as wide as the Mississippi.

"Mrs. Winston, welcome indeed to *The Langham*. We have the best suite for you and your stepdaughter."

"I should surely think you have, sir," returned Mrs. Winston. "We reserved it well in advance. I'm determined that Madelina should have the best London has to offer."

The Manager glanced towards Madelina and did a double take. What a beauty!

Madelina hardly noticed. Her head was tilted as she counted the buttons on the Manager's jacket. Then her eyes swung up to the huge chandelier above with its globes of yellow light.

The two guests were shown to their first floor suite, which was as satisfactory as Mrs. Winston had hoped.

She was in London, as the doorman had suspected, to launch her stepdaughter of nineteen into English Society and at the same time catch an aristocratic title.

She had no illusions about herself. She was a mere upstart, the daughter of a grain merchant from Kansas, who had been lucky enough to marry into money.

But she nurtured a burning ambition to be related to Nobility. And Madelina was her gambling chip.

Madelina's father had died three years before and, though he had left his widow, Mrs. Winston, comfortable, he had left his lovely daughter a veritable fortune.

Mrs. Winston knew only too well that there were many impoverished aristocrats here in England who would espouse a baboon, if there was money in the match!

And Madelina was no baboon!

She had hoped to encounter the odd Duke or Earl on board *The Boston Queen*, a smart Liner that had carried her and Madelina to England, but had been out of luck.

Anyway a shipboard liaison might not have proved the best start. Better by far for Madelina to meet up with the English aristocracy on their own ground, where their virtues might be easily displayed and their vices disguised.

Madelina had no inkling of her stepmother's plans.

She had agreed to come here to England because she was interested in tracing her English lineage, of which she knew very little.

Her father had left his native land when he was just twenty-two years of age. He had rarely spoken about his background except to hint that his own mother, Madelina's grandmother, had been related to the aristocracy.

Madelina's paternal grandparents had died long ago and she was hoping that she would be able to locate some relations who were still living.

She had no one in America, as her mother had been an orphan. The only family she had that she knew of was Mrs. Winston and she was not really family at all!

Madelina moved to the window to gaze out.

She strained on tiptoe to see who had just stepped out of a private carriage. It was a tall slender gentleman in a top hat and black cape and carrying a silver-tipped cane.

He paused on the pavement to chat with the bellboy and Madelina was able to appraise him at her leisure. He had a haughty aquiline profile and a lock of very dark hair strayed onto his forehead from under the brim of his hat.

She wondered idly what his business was at *The Langham* and guessed that he was here to drink champagne and smoke cigars.

He raised his hat to a young woman who passed him on the steps and Madelina felt a sting of envy.

He looked so very handsome and suave, her first sight of the perfect English gentleman! He could have stepped straight out of one of those English novelettes she read.

"What are you looking at?" Mrs. Winston asked.

"Oh, London," replied Madelina, withdrawing from the window.

But Mrs. Winston hurried past her to stare down at the street.

"Well, Madelina Winston, you amaze me! Keeping such a specimen all to yourself."

Madelina blushed.

"Really, Stepmama, I was hardly doing that."

"He's a fine figure. Do you suppose he's an Earl or a Duke?" Mrs. Winston burbled on.

"I would not know what an Earl or a Duke looked like," replied Madelina truthfully. "I mean – do they look different from other gentleman?"

"They have *Blue Blood*," retorted her stepmother. "Of course they look different."

A sudden image of a large blue face floated into Madelina's mind and she gave a giggle.

"I suppose I will be able to tell who they are in future when I meet them."

"I certainly hope so," replied Mrs. Winston. "It's as important as being able to tell the difference between a counterfeit coin and the real thing."

Madelina had no time to ponder this conundrum, as a gentle knock came at the door. They turned as a maid entered to unpack their trunks.

Mrs. Winston surveyed her critically.

"What are you called?" she asked.

"Beth, ma'am," she replied with an awkward bob.

"Have you worked at *The Langham* for some time? Do you know the clientele?"

Beth nodded a 'yes' to both questions.

Without any more ado, Mrs. Winston beckoned her to the window and commanded that she look out.

"What am I looking for, ma'am?" asked Beth.

"The gentleman there, Beth," replied Mrs. Winston, pointing. "Has he *Blue Blood*?"

Madelina blushed for her stepmother, while Beth looked flustered.

"Beg your pardon, ma'am?"

"Do you know if he's a Duke or an Earl or a Lord?"

Beth dutifully peered through the glass again.

"Oh, no, he ain't any of them. That's Mr. Oliver or rather, Mr. de Burge. He's a fine gentleman. He meets his friends here of an evenin' before goin' to the theatre. He's ever so popular at *The Langham*, he is."

But Mrs. Winston had lost interest.

"*Mr.* de Burge merely," she sniffed.

Madelina and Beth continued to gaze down. Mr. Oliver de Burge had turned from the bellboy and was now conversing with a tall lady in a fox fur stole.

"Lady Kitty Villers," murmured Beth helpfully.

Madelina leaned closer to the window. The tall lady was very elegant with a long nose and violent red lips.

Madelina felt a pang of envy at the familiarity with which she laid a hand on Mr. de Burge's arm.

"Are they – related?" she ventured to ask Beth.

"No, miss, but she's often in his party. Now her father, he be an aristocrat. He's an Earl, he is."

It was said loudly for Mrs. Winston's benefit, but she had gone into the bedroom.

Beth saw Madelina's luggage by the door.

"Shall I unpack your trunk, miss?" she offered.

"Best attend to my stepmother first," said Madelina, without turning.

She heard Beth tap on the bedroom door and then she was alone.

Gently she opened the window to see if Mr. Oliver de Burge and his beautiful companion were still below.

They were and Madelina pushed the curtain aside. How she wished that she could hear what they were saying. But then suppose that he was saying something that she, Madelina, did not want to hear? Suppose that he was complimenting Lady Kitty on her dress or her hairstyle?

Suppose he was praising her beautiful eyes or her complexion?

If only he could see *me*, she reflected. If only he would look up and catch sight of me!

To her consternation, Oliver de Burge did exactly that. At least he raised his head and stared upwards. The sun was setting and its dying gleam appeared to alight with special attention on Mr. de Burge's features.

Madelina drank in the sight and his face was, for a brief moment, hers and hers alone. She saw his strong dark eyebrows, one arched disdainfully high.

She noted his eyes, which even at this distance she could make out were black with heavy lids. Never had she noted so much about any man without being introduced.

He was not, alas, observing her in a like manner. His gaze had settled on the spire of a nearby Church, where a large bird perched high above the clamour of the City.

Could it be a falcon from Regents Park? Madelina watched it keenly as if through his eyes. She followed its progress as it opened its wings and rose to fly away.

When she looked down, it was in time to see Mr. de Burge take Lady Kitty Villers's arm and escort her up the steps and into the hotel.

Madelina let the curtain drop back into place.

She then stood staring at her dim reflection in the mirror. What would Oliver de Burge have seen if he *had* looked her way?

She had often been told that she was beautiful, but she had never really believed it, not in the way that Lady Kitty Villers obviously believed that *she* was beautiful!

She thought her own complexion a little too pink, too like a baby. Her eyes were too large and gave her, she felt, a rather startled expression.

Her hairstyle was surely out of date for this great City. And all her clothes, the height of fashion in Albany, suddenly seemed horribly dated as well.

She had never really cared how she looked before, but now it seemed that nothing about her was right.

Mrs. Winston opened her bedroom door and called,

"You should now think about dressing for dinner, Madelina. I'm sending Beth in to open your trunk."

"There is nothing I want to wear – nothing!" cried Madelina. "I don't like any of those dresses anymore."

Mrs. Winston came into the room, astonished. Her stepdaughter's lack of interest in her own appearance had always been a grave disappointment to her.

"You chose what to bring with you, dear girl."

Madelina threw herself onto the sofa.

"I know I did. But I just did not realise how old-fashioned they would seem here."

Mrs. Winston put her hand to her breast.

"Well, my dear, I'd be only too delighted to take you round the stores for a whole new wardrobe. Why not? It's not as if you don't have the funds. We can dress you to look as well as any young lady in this magnificent City."

Madelina glanced at her stepmother and away. She did not dare voice the question that trembled on her lips.

Could Mrs. Winston even dress her to look as good as Lady Kitty, daughter of an Earl and companion of the most romantic-looking man in England?

*

Mrs. Winston's eyes darted hither and thither over dinner, searching the adjoining tables as if each might sport a flag indicating '*Blue Bloods* are supping here'.

Madelina, however, kept her gaze firmly fixed on the large gilt wall mirror facing her. She was not regarding herself in its shining depths, but she was busy watching the reflections of Mr. de Burge and Lady Kitty Villers where they sat with two friends at a table nearby.

She noticed that many fellow diners on their way in or out of the dining room stopped to greet them.

One was a rotund gentleman in a tartan waistcoat, an unlit cigar in his fist. Feet planted wide on the carpet, he seemed to be regaling the de Burge party with details of a shoot and some of his words hit the air like,

"Buckshot, fine birds, brought down, fifty of them myself. The Prince of Wales bagged a hundred or I'm a French monk!"

Mrs. Winston herself twisted round in her chair as she heard this last expression.

"The Prince of Wales!" she said. "That gentleman knows the Prince of Wales."

She beckoned to a waiter.

"That fellow holding forth there, what's his name?"

The waiter turned his head to follow her gaze.

"It's Tunney Whipps, the Duke of Belmont himself, ma'am. Head of one of the most distinguished families in England," he added with just a slight hint of reprimand at her referring to the Duke as a 'fellow'.

Madelina felt the Duke looked more like a farmer in fancy dress than a member of the aristocracy, but Mrs. Winston was impressed.

"We shall endeavour to cross his path later," she whispered to her stepdaughter.

This plan proved more difficult to pursue than Mrs. Winston thought, as the Duke went to the smoking room, entry to which premises was expressly denied to the ladies.

After supper was over Mrs. Winston hovered in the hotel drawing room in the hope that he or some other *'Blue Blood'* might drop in, but she was to be disappointed.

Madelina was disappointed for other reasons.

Just as soon as Oliver de Burge and his party had finished eating, they had called for a carriage. Madelina wondered if they were going to the opera or the theatre.

She had bitten her lip as she saw him rise first to draw out Lady Kitty's chair.

As Mrs. Winston had chosen to quit their own table a little later, Madelina had the dubious pleasure of passing by Mr. de Burge's party as they waited in the foyer.

She stole a trembling look at Mr. de Burge and was rewarded by an idle return glance as he turned his attention to Lady Kitty's cape.

But what Madelina did not notice was Lady Kitty's cold gaze after her as she walked away.

Now Madelina and Mrs. Winston sat sipping tea in the drawing room, surrounded by wealthy ladies in such a variety of rich colours and fabrics that Madelina felt that she was gazing at a whirling kaleidoscope.

Soon her head was spinning and she gave a yawn that prompted Mrs. Winston to suggest that they retire.

Once in bed, Madelina fell into a deep slumber and even the unattainable Mr. de Burge was quickly forgotten.

*

The following day Mrs. Winston made good on her promise to take Madelina shopping.

Their assault on the shops of Mayfair yielded such spoils that two carriages were needed to carry the packages back to *The Langham.*

This frenzy of spending did not go un-remarked on their return. As a bevy of valets hauled the cargo from the carriage to the foyer and then on up to the Winston's suite, people paused to watch and comment.

One was Tunney, the Duke of Belmont, who had dropped in for a glass of champagne.

Lorgnette raised up to his nose, his ginger whiskers quivered with interest at the sight.

"The matron and her filly must have a pretty penny or two to spare," he commented to no one in particular. "Wonder if they are Americans?"

He then gave a start as he trained his regard on the filly herself, Madelina, who was flushed at the attention that she and her stepmother were receiving.

'Fine bones, good posture there, Tunney!' he told himself. 'And money. Must make myself known.'

Onlookers fell to the side as the Duke of Belmont made his way forward.

"Madam," he said as he bowed politely over Mrs. Winston's hand. "May I offer my services in this delicate operation of yours? A voice of authority, don't you know, can work wonders with these valets. Give 'em a spurt on!"

Mrs. Winston was at once beside herself with joy as she recognised the Duke.

"I do think they could work a little faster, Duke," she confessed, hand to her bosom.

The Duke issued a sharp command and the valets, who had been rather taking their time with the American ladies' packages, began to move a little faster.

The Duke meanwhile suggested that the two ladies join him in the champagne bar.

Mrs. Winston accepted the invitation with alacrity, congratulating herself on the speed with which her dream of mingling with the Nobility had come about.

Madelina was not unwilling to follow suit, for the simple reason that the Duke numbered Mr. Oliver de Burge amongst his acquaintances.

The Duke then ordered two bottles of Perrier Jouet champagne.

"Favourite of a certain celebrated playwright," he said with a wink.

Mrs. Winston, whose knowledge of the theatre was limited, looked at him blankly.

"Well – harrumph," beamed the Duke. "Allow me to raise a toast to the two loveliest ladies to have crossed the ocean in a long time."

Mrs. Winston simpered, but Madelina wrinkled her nose as champagne bubbles attacked her nostrils.

"Charming, so very charming," muttered the Duke, surveying her through his glass.

Mrs. Winston then repressed a shiver of excitement at his admiration for her unwary stepdaughter. Everything was falling so wonderfully into place.

"And where is your estate, Duke?" she asked him.

The Duke tore his reluctant gaze from Madelina.

"In – harrumph – Gloucestershire, madam."

"And the Duchess resides there most of the time?"

The Duke assumed an expression of regret.

"The Duchess stays nowhere, madam, for the very simple reason that she does not exist."

"Well, bless me," cried Mrs. Winston at once, her heart surging in her breast.

This was all proving to be so much easier than she had anticipated.

"A fine gentleman like yourself unmarried! It just ain't – isn't natural."

The Duke sighed again.

"I have the title, madam. I have the land. I have the house. But all that costs a package to run. And at the moment I find myself unable to provide those extra little luxuries that a woman requires, nay, demands!"

His eyes met those of Mrs. Winston with candour and a flash of understanding passed between the two.

"But, Duke," Mrs. Winston then murmured, "who knows what the future may hold?"

The Duke followed her gaze to settle on Madelina, who had been listening with impatience to this exchange.

She had no interest in titles, land or houses.

She was wondering when she might introduce the topic of Mr. Oliver de Burge.

"Perhaps you and your daughter would care to visit Belmont Hall?" suggested the Duke.

"Stepdaughter," Mrs. Winston corrected the Duke, secretly hugging herself at the invitation. "And oh, we'd be delighted to stay at Belmont, wouldn't we, Madelina?"

Madelina turned and cast her large amber eyes on the Duke, whose whiskers gave a tremor of desire.

"But we have only just arrived in London," said Madelina cautiously.

If she left *The Langham* now, when would she ever set eyes on Mr. Oliver de Burge again?

Mrs. Winston, however, would brook no resistance. She was determined to grasp this unexpected opportunity, in case it was the last. And she was not the only American matron here seeking a titled gentleman for her charge.

"We'll stay on in London for a week or so, during which time I'll look for a house to rent in Mayfair," she declared. "Then we'd love to come to Belmont Hall."

The Duke gave a chortle of pleasure.

"Done, then!

Madelina cast about for other excuses.

"But if we are closeted in the country, how will I make enquiries about my relations?"

"Your relations have been anonymous for nineteen years," said Mrs. Winston. "Another month won't matter."

"A month?"

"It will be good for you to see a stretch of England, Miss Winston," came in the Duke quickly. "And if you are worried about the isolation, well, my distant cousin will be there. He's coming to look at the horses. Thoroughbreds. He may well purchase one or two from me. Unless things suddenly look up – "

The Duke here heaved a heavy sigh, but Madelina was not listening.

 Mrs. Winston frowned and drained her glass.

"I think Madelina is rather tired with all the rush this morning," she said, rising. "If you'll excuse us."

The Duke hauled himself up and gave a bow.

"Certainly, dear ladies. I am off to Gloucestershire tomorrow, but I shall leave the directions for you with the concierge. In two weeks' time I shall expect the pleasure of your company at Belmont!"

Madelina was in turmoil as she and her stepmother made their way to the grand staircase of *The Langham*.

She had not managed to bring Oliver de Burge's name into the chat with the Duke, who was now about to drive off to his estate.

The longing that surged in her breast at the thought of that gentleman, who had no idea that she existed, was new to her and she had no past experience to cope with it.

She had seen him and his image was engraved on her heart. That was all she knew.

The two ladies reached the staircase. Mrs. Winston mounted ahead, puffing a little with each step.

Madelina, following her, stopped in her tracks as she heard Oliver de Burge's name pronounced behind her.

She turned. He had obviously been hailed just as he entered the hotel and, as he stood below, an animated gentleman interposed between himself and the stairs.

14

De Burge had removed his hat and his thick dark hair fell about his collar. His forehead was visible, pale and high above those black eyes.

He was now listening courteously to the man who had hailed him, but his attention was not held.

His gaze wandered, over the man's shoulder and up the staircase, where it fell on Madelina, standing still as a statue looking down.

A crease appeared between his eyebrows as if he was trying to place her. His eyes then ran up and down her frame with an appreciation that both thrilled and alarmed her, for it was haughty and impersonal.

Her fingers tightened on the gilt banister as his gaze lifted again to her face.

She could not see what he saw.

A girl whose eyes were unaccountably shining and whose cheeks were flushed as a red rose and whose breast was heaving beneath her velvet bodice.

She longed to swoon, to tumble those few steps into his manly arms and confess her feelings to him.

Mr. de Burge, alas, was only momentarily intrigued and he gave a little nod as of greeting before turning back to his friend.

"What *are* you doing there?" came Mrs. Winston's irritated voice, a step or two above Madelina.

She had reached the top of the first flight and then looked back to see her stepdaughter mesmerised below her.

Madelina hurried on up, blushing.

"I-I happened to see Mr. de Burge below – " she began to explain, but her voice trailed away.

Not having been introduced to him, there was really no excuse for her to stand there hoping for his attention.

Mrs. Winston threw up her hands.

"Then, of what interest is Mr. de Burge to us? He may be the richest man in London for all I know, but he is a nobody."

"How can you say that, Stepmama?" she said in a half-whisper, aware that Mr. de Burge might still be just a flight of stairs below. "He is so handsome and obviously distinguished and very popular at *The Langham*."

Mrs. Winston threw a troubled look at Madelina. The sooner she whisked the girl away from *The Langham* the better.

"How you do go on," she replied, catching hold of Madelina's elbow and manoeuvring her towards their suite.

"The first gentleman you see turns your head like the gullible fool you are. London is full of such characters, I can promise you. You've spent too much time with your head in a book and I daresay you'd fall in love with every handsome man you saw if I didn't discourage you."

"And I have never seen one as handsome as Mr. de Burge," countered Madelina with conviction.

"Oh, such balderdash, my dear. Why, the Duke of Belmont has a far more memorable appearance."

Madelina then turned upon her stepmother such an expression of scorn that she was quite silenced.

It was obviously going to need all her ingenuity to acclimatise Madelina to the idea of marriage with the Duke and marriage was on the cards, of that she was convinced. The Duke was broke and Madelina was the answer to his prayers and his title was the answer to *her* prayers.

She would put paid to this romantic nonsense of her stepdaughter or her name was not Abigail Winston!

CHAPTER TWO

In fact Mrs. Winston need not have troubled herself so much about Mr. de Burge, for he did not reappear at the hotel during the rest of the time that they were there.

Every evening Madelina watched out for him and every evening she was painfully disappointed.

It is, however, in the nature of sudden afflictions of the heart that the image of the beloved fades.

By the time that they had moved into their rented house in Wigmore Street, Madelina had to admit to herself that she could not recall the precise set of Mr. Oliver de Burge's features.

It was Beth who eventually informed her that Mr. de Burge had gone to Deauville for the end of the Season, the movements of visitors to *The Langham* being common gossip below stairs.

Madelina had become quite fond of Beth. Seeing this and realising that her stepdaughter was rather lonely for company of her own age, Mrs. Winston offered Beth a position as lady's maid.

Beth was only too delighted to escape the drudgery of *The Langham* and accepted gladly.

Once they had securely settled into the flat, Mrs. Winston began planning the trip to Belmont Hall.

She had not alluded to the Duke's invitation since that evening in the champagne bar. Better to wait, she felt, until Madelina was well away from *The Langham Hotel* and memories of Mr. de Burge.

It was an unexpected boon when he had removed himself from the scene. She was convinced that Madelina would forget him entirely and the way would be open for the Duke to win her affections.

When at last Mrs. Winston did broach the subject of Belmont, she found Madelina surprisingly willing.

If she had suspected her stepmother's plotting, she might have refused the trip, but as it was, she did not care whether she was in London or in the country.

Her only interest now was in tracing her father's long lost family and a month's wait would not hurt.

*

It was the last week in September when finally Mrs. Winston, Madelina and Beth took the train for Gloucester, where the Duke's carriage would be waiting for them.

They travelled First Class, even Beth, although the maid did not accompany them to the dining car for lunch.

Mrs. Winston, taking her seat, inclined her head to a lady passenger sitting alone at the table across the aisle.

This lady then returned her greeting. She had silver hair, which her large feathered hat failed to conceal.

She introduced herself as Lady Bamber, widow of Lord Bamber of Cressy Manor in Gloucestershire.

Mrs. Winston was naturally excited to be meeting yet another member of the aristocracy that she completely failed to properly introduce herself and Madelina.

"Why," she gushed instead, "we're ever so happy to make your acquaintance! We ourselves are now visiting Europe from America and we're travelling to stay with the Duke of Belmont. Do you know him?"

Lady Bamber's eyes flicked from Mrs. Winston to Madelina and back and, although her reply was courteous, there was an unmistakable stiffening of her manner.

"The Duke of Belmont was a friend of my late husband," she said.

"And a very fine gentleman, the Duke!" ventured Mrs. Winston.

"And a gullible one, I am afraid," commented Lady Bamber coolly.

Folding her napkin, she rose and made her excuses to a discomfited Mrs. Winston, who had not supposed that her intention for Madelina and the Duke to be so apparent.

Deciding that it was best to portray herself as the injured party, Mrs Winston waved a dismissive hand.

"How stuck-up these aristocrats can be!"

Madelina lowered her head.

Lady Bamber had looked so friendly at first. What can have made her change her attitude towards them? Was it because they were American?

By the time the train had pulled in at Gloucester, however, the incident was all but forgotten.

The Duke of Belmont's carriage was waiting and, if its axles were coated with mud and its upholstery smelling of must, it was still a very handsome vehicle with a Coat of Arms gratifyingly emblazoned on its side panels.

Belmont Hall, when it hove into view, quite took their breath away.

It was vast!

Mrs. Winston was rather crushed at the many signs of neglect, but this soon changed to her satisfaction at how impoverished and therefore needy the Duke must be.

Madelina did not notice that the steps leading up to the front door were cracked or that the iron balustrade was rusty and in need of paint.

To her the house was history incarnate, a place of dreams, and if it was not that the Duke of Belmont resided here, it would have been perfection itself.

The Duke received his guests with great aplomb. He had been in the habit of borrowing against the estate so that he could 'put on a good show' and he was not inclined to stint for a young lady whom he was anxious to impress.

So let the stepmother wonder where the money to entertain came from and she and the lovely 'filly' should be just overwhelmed with splendour.

So against a background of peeling tartan wallpaper and threadbare tapestries, his guests were prevailed upon to partake of ice-cold champagne in crystal flutes and dainty pastry cases of caviar.

Although a fine dust rose from the sofas when they sat down, the fire in the big marble hearth burned fiercely.

"September in the country is a very different matter to September in London," said the Duke, planting himself four-square before the blazing fire.

"It's indeed chilly in here," agreed Mrs. Winston.

Madelina cheeks now flushed the colour of tea rose. This was both from the immense warmth of the fire and the intense scrutiny of the Duke.

His eyes rolled in her direction like brown marbles, alighting now on her long neck, now on her shapely figure and now on her ankle.

"You, Miss Winston, how do you like Belmont so far?" he asked.

"I find it very – welcoming," she stammered.

"Welcoming!" roared the Duke. "I am famous for it. We shall have a big party. Would you like that? Eh?"

"I am s-sure I would," murmured Madelina.

The Duke gave a nod.

"I'll invite a few of my neighbours."

"We met one of them on the train," came in Mrs. Winston cautiously. "A certain Lady Bamber?"

She could not be sure, but the Duke's florid face seemed to grow redder still.

"Ah, yes. After Lord Bamber died, she and I, that is to say, I would have offered, but she wasn't so inclined."

From this admission Madelina understood that he had considered proposing to the widowed Lady Bamber, but his attentions had not been encouraged.

'Good for Lady Bamber,' thought Madelina with a suppressed giggle.

The lady was at least twenty years older than him.

"And why would he want to marry her?" whispered Madelina to her stepmother.

Mrs. Winston, who could well guess why the Duke had wished to marry a wealthy widow, gave a shrug.

"Out of sympathy, perhaps, or loneliness. It cannot be much fun to be marooned down here on your own."

The Duke turned to hold his hands out to the fire.

"I'll have my footman show you to your rooms," he said over his shoulder. "Dinner is at eight sharp."

Madelina found her bedroom to be less shabby than the rest of Belmont. The walls were all lined with yellow Chinese silk that had somehow stood the test of time.

Throwing open the casement window, she stared at an oyster-coloured full moon.

A tawny owl swooped out from the trees and back again and it reminded Madelina of the bird on the steeple spire in London, the bird that Oliver de Burge had noticed.

From there it was but an instant in the moonlight to summon up the ghost of the man she had admired from a distance.

'Where was he tonight?' she wondered.

She changed into one of her new gowns for dinner and hardly glanced at herself in the mirror. What did she care how she looked, when there was no gentleman here to admire her but the faintly ridiculous Duke of Belmont!

The dining room was draughty, but the Duke had spared no expense when it came to the dinner itself.

There was a first course of baked scallops followed by bouillon. Then in came a salmon on a silver platter with potatoes and garden vegetables.

There was a dish of roast quail with greengages and freshly baked bread.

Dessert was steamed plum pudding.

The two guests were plied with wine between each course and Madeira at the end.

Mrs. Winston partook of everything with as much gusto as the Duke, until her face flamed like a lobster.

Madelina looked on with growing distaste as her stepmother seemed to throw caution to the wind.

"Why, I fancy I could stay here at Belmont for a hundred years," Mrs. Winston gushed.

"That could be easily arranged," returned the Duke. "Just a little *quid pro quo* is all it takes."

Madelina blinked. What did the Duke mean by that '*quid pro quo*'?

Mrs. Winston meanwhile gave a shrug.

"I can deliver the '*quid*', Duke, don't you worry."

The Duke twiddled one of his whiskers, the tips of which were damp and discoloured from their tendency to straggle into every dish set before him.

He wondered if Mrs. Winston understood the pun she had made, since '*quid*' was such a London expression.

'She is a sharp enough old bird,' he decided, 'to have picked up that slang up at *The Langham*'.

"Never count your pheasants till they're in the bag, madam," he observed. "That's my philosophy."

Mrs. Winston, much to Madelina's surprise, then began to splutter with laughter.

"Pheasants! Oh, my. Is that how you see us poor helpless creatures? Dumb feathered creatures. Ha ha ha!"

Madelina put down her glass.

"If you will excuse me, Stepmama – Duke."

The Duke's hand dropped from his whiskers.

"You're leaving us? So soon?"

"I am very tired."

Mrs. Winston waved a hand at her.

"Oh, go on to bed if you will. Don't worry, Duke. You and I have matters to discuss."

The Duke then rose in his chair to bid Madelina a reluctant goodnight.

She hurried from the room with relief. Had her stepmother and the Duke lost their wits? What on earth had they to talk about there at the table?

She was making her way to the staircase when she heard the sound of hoofs outside. Who was now arriving at Belmont at this hour?

She expected to hear someone dismount to pull the entrance bell, but the rider went galloping on. Obviously it was someone who knew Belmont and was making for the stable yard.

Madelina went to the stairs and began to climb.

She had reached the landing when she heard voices echoing along the corridor.

"Is my cousin here?" someone called out.

The Duke had indeed said that his second cousin might appear at Belmont, but Madelina had not imagined that a relative of the Duke might have such an attractively deep and manly voice.

Cautiously she peered over the banister.

At the sight of the figure below her heart seized up within her. She could not mistake that tall slender frame, that abundance of dark hair.

As Mr. Oliver de Burge threw off his cape and hat, she sank down in a swoon on the upper landing step and pressed her suddenly fevered brow against the banisters.

Surely it was Fate that he of all men in the world should reappear in her life like this? He hardly knew that she existed, but now she would be able to meet him at last.

And there was nothing Mrs. Winston or Lady Kitty Villers or even the Duke could do about it.

*

Mrs. Winston looked decidedly sick at breakfast the next morning. Madelina sat opposite her and then ventured to enquire whether her stepmother was quite well.

"As well as can be expected in the circumstances," Mrs. Winston snapped.

"What circumstances, Stepmama?"

Mrs. Winston looked exasperated.

"Oh, don't you play the innocent with me. I mean the situation is not as propitious as it was. You've heard that Mr. de Burge, the object of your interest in London, arrived here last night?"

Madelina did not meet her stepmother's stare.

"I-I knew that, yes," she admitted.

Mrs. Winston sniffed.

"He stole into the house, it appears, just after you retired. Didn't so much as put his head round the drawing room door to say hello to his relation."

Madelina looked up quickly.

"He is – the Duke's cousin, then?"

"He is indeed. Come here to give his opinion on the Duke's horses." Mrs. Winston gave a stifled snort. "Let's hope he doesn't want to give his opinion on you as well!"

"Stepmama!" Madelina was shocked.

"You're to keep out of his way, do you hear?" Mrs. Winston warned. "I know his sort. Man about town. The Duke has told me all."

"Man about town?" wondered Madelina. "What do you mean by that, Stepmama?"

"It means he whispers sweet nothings to any pretty girl that takes his fancy. It means cards and the races and expensive gentlemen's Clubs."

Madelina lowered her head. This might be all too true, but hurt her to the quick.

But she meant to give Mr. de Burge the benefit of the doubt. She would surely have the opportunity to get to know him a little if he stayed at Belmont for a few days.

Unless – and her heart gave a little lurch of anxiety – unless he was only here for the day?

"Do you know if he is staying long?" she asked.

"What is it to you, then?" demanded Mrs. Winston. "I thought that coming away, visiting the Duke and seeing Belmont, would put all that nonsense out of your head. Mr. de Burge is an opportunist. He is after his cousin's estate and he'll put a spanner in the works, mark my words."

"Spanner in the works?" Madelina looked puzzled.

Mrs. Winston poured an angry stream of milk into her tea.

"It's something I heard Beth say. It means – he'll ruin it all, our little visit here."

"I don't see why."

"Oh, don't you?" Mrs. Winston turned fiercely on her. "I'll tell you why. He'll stir up all that nonsense in you and you won't take notice of your host – the Duke."

"I would never neglect any courtesy towards the Duke," declared Madelina. "I am very well aware of his kindness in inviting us here."

She might have gone on, but the door behind her stepmother opened and the Duke stepped in.

Madelina felt a rush of disappointment, as she had been hoping for another face.

The Duke heaved himself into a chair and beckoned over the breakfast maid.

"Kippers!" he then ordered. "Make it a shoal! And scrambled eggs, fresh from the hen."

Mrs. Winston gave an appreciative smile.

"A shoal! Scrambled eggs from the hen! What a tease you are, Duke."

The Duke met Mrs. Winston's gaze.

Their little talk last night had come to a satisfactory conclusion. Mrs. Winston had given him full permission to pursue her stepdaughter and promising to exert her own influence on Madelina as far as was possible.

The Duke had no inkling that last night's arrival of his cousin, Mr. de Burge, threw the plan into jeopardy and the anxious furrows on Mrs. Winston's brow puzzled him.

"I trust breakfast is to your liking?" he asked.

"You treat us like royalty!" said Mrs. Winston, but in a pre-occupied fashion. "By the way, I heard from our maid that your cousin arrived last night."

"He did indeed," agreed the Duke. "Didn't make his presence known to me, ma'am, until you had retired. Didn't want to interrupt us."

"Is he – joining us this morning?" asked Madelina casually, although her heart raced to hear the answer.

"He's not the sort of man to take his breakfast in bed," returned the Duke. "Why, here he is now, I believe."

But Madelina had heard footsteps approaching even while the Duke spoke and her gaze was on the door as Mr. de Burge stepped into the room.

In an instant the image that had faded in her mind surged vividly forth like a developing photograph.

Just how could she have forgotten that disdainfully arched eyebrow, those black eyes and that haughty aquiline nose?

Oliver de Burge did not immediately come into the room, but stood still languidly surveying the scene.

His eye roved over the occupants at the table and settled somewhat quizzically on Madelina, who felt a blush rise to her cheeks.

"Ladies," he said politely. "I do so hope that I am not disturbing your breakfast chatter?"

Madelina started. Did he intend a slight with that word 'chatter'? Mrs. Winston obviously thought so, as her bosom fluffed up like that of a turkey hen.

"We are just having a *conversation*," she stressed acidly, " which you are by all means welcome to join."

His upper lip quivered with suppressed amusement, although he bowed with a grave face.

"Thank you. I shall. You are, Mrs. Winston?"

She graciously acknowledged that he was correct.

"We were staying at *The Langham* at the same time as yourself, although we were not introduced. And this," she added, "is my stepdaughter, Miss Madelina Winston."

He bowed without comment and then sat down.

Madelina felt crushed. He had shown no interest in her whatsoever, beyond his first mildly puzzled glance and she bent her head, desperate to conceal her expression.

Why had she never learned to mask her feelings like every successful young lady on the social circuit?

"A roll?"

His voice startled her. She looked up to see that he was proffering a basket of warm rolls.

Madelina reached out her hand only to realise with dismay that it was shaking and then hastily withdrew it.

"Thank you, no," she replied.

Mrs. Winston was watching Madelina closely.

"Maybe you have finished your breakfast," she said sharply. "In which case you may leave the table."

The Duke stepped in with a protest.

"But she hasn't yet tasted our famous hot chocolate. Nobody makes it like our cook here at Belmont."

Madelina was grateful for this. As much as Mr. de Burge unsettled her, she did not want to leave his presence.

He meanwhile took it on himself to pour her a cup of piping hot chocolate and she could not help but admire his long slender fingers curled round the handle of the jug.

Mrs. Winston at once decided on another tack, one that would warn him not to trespass on the Duke's interest.

"You are a most attentive host, Duke. But you are in *great* need of a hostess."

"To be sure!" agreed the Duke. "To be sure. But the kind of gel I'd like doesn't grow on trees."

Mrs. Winston's eyes gleamed.

"And what kind of 'gel' is it you like? Do tell us."

The Duke, now interpreting this as encouragement to announce his interest in her stepdaughter, gave a wink.

"Why, you know – Miss Madelina here is the sort of filly I really admire."

Madelina was just speechless. Her eyes met those of Oliver de Burge for a moment and she quailed at their cool sardonic expression.

Did he think she welcomed such crudely expressed comments? She looked away in confusion, while de Burge turned to address the Duke.

"There is some 'filly' or another anxious to arouse interest such as yours arriving here on every tide, cousin. Not that I count the charming Miss Madelina among their number, of course. But it seems a veritable 'ocean of love' flows between our two countries these days."

Mrs. Winston then gave a splutter of outrage, while Madelina blenched.

There was no mistaking the note of contempt in de Burge's voice, though at the same time she was not entirely sure of his meaning. Girls arriving here on every tide? *An ocean of love*?

The Duke was clearly annoyed by his insinuation.

"Come, man!" he grunted. "I'm no easy bait. But I know what I like and I know what I need. And that's an end to it. Will you take a look at the stables now?"

Mr. de Burge, though he had barely eaten anything, rose. With a curt nod to Mrs. Winston and Madelina, he followed the disgruntled Duke from the room.

"Well!" exploded Mrs. Winston as the door closed. "Now you can see the true nature of that creature!"

Madelina stared down at her plate.

"Stepmama, what did he mean?"

"When, dear?"

"When he was talking about American girls and 'an ocean of love'."

Mrs. Winston fell into a fit of coughing. Madelina looked on, only responding when she asked for water.

She rose and poured some into a china teacup.

As she did so, she glanced towards the window to see that a light carriage, drawn by two high-stepping roans, was rattling towards the house.

The sight had arrested the Duke and Mr. de Burge as well, for they stood watching the approaching vehicle.

Mrs. Winston gulped from the teacup and sat back.

"I must have swallowed a bone in the kedgeree."

Madelina regarded her stepmother.

"But what did Mr. de Burge mean?" she persisted.

"Oh dear, how you do discomfort me," complained Mrs. Winston, picking up her napkin and folding it.

"I think he meant that a lot of American girls come to England looking to marry a – a titled gentleman."

Mrs. Winston then fanned her face with the napkin, avoiding Madelina's eyes.

Madelina moved slowly away. It was horribly clear to her now. Mr. de Burge must think that *she* was one of those girls, although he had politely suggested otherwise.

Perhaps he thought, and she gave a silent groan of misery, that she was setting her cap at the Duke.

From that thought to the next took an instant only.

She might not be setting her cap at the Duke, but her stepmother definitely was – on her behalf!

Her unhappy musings brought her to the window.

She saw that the carriage had pulled up in front of the house and a footman was in the process of handing out the occupant, while the Duke and Mr. de Burge stood by.

With a start Madelina saw that the new arrival was none other than the very Lady Bamber who had snubbed herself and Mrs. Winston on the train yesterday.

The reason for that snub seemed clear now, she too assumed that Madelina was a title-seeker.

Madelina watched as the Duke and Mr. de Burge greeted Lady Bamber. The Duke then escorted her up the steps and they engaged in animated conversation.

Mr. de Burge meanwhile had strolled away towards the stables, no doubt to inspect the Duke's horses.

Madelina turned from the window, half-expecting a summons. In this she was not mistaken as within minutes a servant appeared and came across to her.

"The Duke and Lady Bamber now request your attendance in the library, ma'am."

Mrs. Winston regarded the servant with a frown.

"Did the Duke ask for me as well?"

"No, ma'am. Just Miss Madelina."

"Oh." Mrs. Winston looked most affronted, but did not object. "Then you'd better run along, Madelina."

Madelina set out with apprehension.

She certainly did not relish meeting this long-time acquaintance of the Duke, who had clearly formed such an unfavourable impression of herself and her stepmother on the train. But a refusal would not be good manners.

The servant opened the library door and ushered her in.

Lady Bamber was there alone. Somewhat surprised at this, Madelina dropped a curtsey.

Before she could rise Lady Bamber had rushed over and seized her in such a fierce embrace that she was nearly smothered against the older woman's ample bosom.

"Welcome to our pretty little corner of England, *cousin*," she heard Lady Bamber say over her head.

Madelina drew back in astonishment.

'Was this 'cousin' then a common form of address in England?' she reflected.

Lady Bamber was beaming at her.

"Ah, yes. Now, at closer inspection, I can see your father in you. It's a miracle!"

"M-my father?" repeated Madelina in amazement.

Lady Bamber drew Madelina to a chair.

"I am so overwhelmed to find you," she murmured, clasping Madelina's hands in her own. "So completely overwhelmed. You see, my dear, I have just realised that you are my relation. My only surviving relation!"

"You – are?"

Lady Bamber nodded.

"My dear child, I am your father's first cousin, his sister Harriet's daughter. The siblings lost touch after your father left to go to America. We heard from other sources that he had married and now had a daughter, Madelina."

She paused to catch her breath before continuing,

"So when I reached my home yesterday and found a note from the Duke inviting me to meet his American guests, a Mrs. Winston and her stepdaughter, Madelina, I hardly dared hope! I realised then that you must be the two ladies I had met on the train, because your stepmother had said that your destination was Belmont."

Madelina, who could hardly believe what she was hearing, took up the one point she felt she could reply to.

"But you did not seem to approve of me – on the train."

Lady Bamber looked embarrassed.

"I may not have approved of what I believed to be your stepmother's motivation in visiting Belmont."

"Her motivation?"

A shadow crossed Madelina's face as she recalled Mr. de Burge's comments about American girls and titles.

Lady Bamber noticed the shadow at once and then, misinterpreting its cause, privately kicked herself.

She would not malign the stepmother to Madelina at any cost as it might mean the loss of a relation she was only too delighted to have miraculously discovered.

Gingerly Lady Bamber tucked away a stray curl from Madelina's face. The gesture was so motherly that Madelina could not suppress a sob from escaping her lips.

"You are – really my father's cousin?"

"If his name was Bertram Carver Winston, then I most definitely am, my dear. I thought that I was all that was left of our family. Until today."

With a cry, Madelina then threw herself into Lady Bamber's arms.

She had come to England with one ambition – to find out about her father's lineage.

And right here, in the unlikely setting of Belmont Hall, she had found the answer to her prayer!

CHAPTER THREE

Mrs. Winston was fetched to be informed of this unexpected development.

When she learned of the connection between this lady and her stepdaughter, she had to be helped to a seat.

Her obvious concern that she might not henceforth exert total influence over Madelina was tempered by the fact that, with no effort on her part, she was already related by marriage to an actual *Lady*.

Her face clouded as she remembered the reason for Lady Bamber's original snub. She had not liked the idea that her old acquaintance, the Duke, was the target of title-hunters. How would she feel about it now?

Timidly, she cleared her throat, intending to broach the subject of the Duke's interest in her stepdaughter. But Lady Bamber's next few words negated the need.

"It's such a pity," she sighed, "that I have to leave you almost at once!"

"L-leave?" Madelina's face fell.

"I am scheduled to travel to France this afternoon," Lady Bamber replied. "I came down from London to issue instructions to my household and to collect my passport."

"Do you *have* to go?" cried Madelina.

Lady Bamber gave a wan smile.

"I am afraid I do. My late husband's mother is in Paris. She is ninety and failing fast. I must see her before she dies."

"Of course, you must visit her," Madelina said.

"There are affairs to put in order," Lady Bamber went on, "so I will probably be away for a month at least."

"A month!" wailed Madelina.

"But I shall be back for Christmas," Lady Bamber assured her. "Which I hope you and your stepmother will spend with me at Cressy Manor."

Madelina, though disappointed to have discovered a relation only to lose her again, gamely clapped her hands.

"Oh, we would love to, wouldn't we, Stepmama?"

"Certainly we would." Mrs. Winston answered her, although her mind was elsewhere.

She was calculating what might transpire during the time Lady Bamber was away. It was nice to have a Lady in the family, but such a title could not compare to a Duke.

Was a month long enough to convince Madelina to marry the Duke and have the Wedding over and done with before Lady Bamber returned?

For Mrs. Winston could not be certain that Lady Bamber would approve of the marriage. She might have a different attitude to a so-called 'title-seeker' from America if that seeker was her own relation.

In addition the Duke had once proposed to Lady Bamber herself and so it would be for the best if it was all concluded without Lady Bamber's involvement.

This trip of hers to France was a God-send!

Having extracted a definite promise that Madelina and Mrs. Winston would spend Christmas with her, Lady Bamber made her reluctant departure.

Lady Bamber had told the Duke of her suspicion that his young guest might be a relation and when he saw the two together it was clear that this had proved the case.

"Capital, capital!" he then said, rubbing his hands together with a glee that made Mrs. Winston thoughtful.

"Has Lady Bamber any children?" she whispered, as she and Madelina hugged each other on the steps below.

"None alive!" replied the Duke in a low voice and he and Mrs. Winston exchanged an understanding glance.

It was in this case easily possible that Lady Bamber might make Madelina her heir. Two fortunes combined, a prospect to make any suitor gleeful.

"I shall write from Paris," Lady Bamber was saying as she kissed Madelina goodbye.

"Please do!" Madelina pleaded.

As the Duke stepped forward to hand Lady Bamber into her carriage, Mr. de Burge appeared on horseback.

He was trying out one of the Duke's horses, a fine black stallion that the Duke himself had never mastered. There had been some struggle between de Burge and the magnificent animal, for the rider's shirt was loosened, his face was flushed and his hair fluttered awry in the breeze.

Madelina, all of whose attention had been on Lady Bamber, was distracted by the sight.

Lady Bamber paused to acknowledge de Burge.

"Mr. de Burge! I hope you will visit Cressy soon."

"I shall indeed," he replied.

"Madelina and Mrs. Winston will be staying too. I have found that the dear girl and I are second cousins. I leave her charming company now with great regret."

Oliver de Burge then turned a somewhat surprised gaze on Madelina. He was but a few feet away and she felt that she would drown in the depths of his dark eyes.

It was as if he saw her for the first time and to her dismay she sensed a blush steal over her cheeks.

"A happy discovery," de Burge murmured.

Lady Bamber turned to climb into her carriage and so did not see the way that de Burge's eyes lingered on her new found cousin.

But Mrs. Winston saw it all. The fellow was putting the same two and two together as the Duke she decided. Marry Madelina and he might acquire a double fortune!

Well, she would soon put a stop to any such notions on his part. She wanted a Duke and nothing less for her stepdaughter and by extension for herself!

While Lady Bamber said her goodbyes to the Duke, Madelina drifted towards de Burge where he sat astride the stallion. Timidly she put out a hand and stroked its nose.

De Burge watched her. His eyes skimmed over her lithe figure, her long limbs and her tiny waist.

When her sleeve slipped down a little to reveal her delicate wrist, something in the sight seemed to disturb Mr. de Burge, for he shifted in the saddle and tightened his jaw.

"Solomon likes you," he said somewhat curtly.

"Solomon?"

Madelina looked up and de Burge started back.

The gold in Madelina's eyes seemed to reflect the gold of autumn itself. He drank in their amber warmth before going on to note her translucent skin, the curve of her ruby lips and the lustrous curls round her forehead.

"Solomon is his name," he said gruffly, as if he was resenting the degree of interest Madelina aroused in him.

Digging his heel into the stallion's side, he turned it around so that Madelina was no longer in his sight and her hand dropped to her side.

The carriage started up and Madelina turned to see Lady Bamber waving at its window and she waved back.

De Burge then trotted alongside the carriage until it reached the trees, when he wheeled Solomon around and headed off towards the woods.

Slowly Madelina turned and followed the Duke and Mrs. Winston into the house.

She was definitely not experienced enough to name the current that had surged between herself and de Burge, but she was aware of a change in his attitude towards her.

No man had ever looked at her quite like that, as if he was drinking in her image.

"Madelina!"

Mrs. Winston's sharp voice disturbed her thoughts and she looked up guiltily.

"What were you thinking of, going so close to that big brute!"

Madelina blinked. There was just something in her stepmother's tone to suggest that 'brute' might not mean the horse alone.

"I-I only wanted to stroke him," she ventured.

The Duke broke in with a laugh.

"Now don't you worry, Mrs. Winston. De Burge can handle anything. He's done more to tame Solomon's temper in an hour than I've been able to do in a year. De Burge is always the Master."

Mrs. Winston gave a low grunt that indicated some continuing displeasure, but said nothing.

It was soon time for luncheon.

There was a dish of baked quails and ham on the bone. Madelina had little appetite, waiting as she was for de Burge to join the party at the table.

When the clock struck midday and there was still no sign of him, she risked her stepmother's ire by daring to ask the Duke where his other guest might be.

"Oh, he will have ridden over to the Earl Villers's estate. He knows the family of old."

Madelina wondered for a short moment why her heart lurched at that name, 'Villers'.

Then a vision of a tall lady in a fox fur stole rushed into her mind. Lady Kitty! Mr. de Burge's companion in London and, remembering her stepmother's contention that de Burge was no more than a 'man about town', she felt her eyes suddenly swim.

The Duke suggested that after luncheon he escort the two ladies on a drive round his extensive estate.

Madelina, not feeling her usual curious self, did not want to, but there was no restraining Mrs. Winston.

Thus it was that at two o'clock the little party of three set out in the Duke's best carriage.

Madelina soon had to concede that it was indeed very pleasant to be driving about in the crisp autumn air.

Belmont Hall itself might be in poor repair, but the land was well tended, due to the many tenant farmers.

Beyond the estate, the carriage entered the village of Belmont with its quaint cottages and ancient Church.

As they drove along the main street, Mrs. Winston was gratified by the numerous signs of deference afforded the Duke with villagers doffing their caps or curtseying.

The Duke ordered his coachman to draw up outside the Church so that his guests could take a look inside.

Madelina liked the musty dim interior with candles flickering in their sconces and stained glass windows.

Then the Duke called anxiously to his guests. He had noticed gathering storm clouds and had decided that it was time to start the journey back to Belmont Hall.

Mrs. Winston and Madelina hurried to the carriage and climbed in, the Duke following them.

As the carriage started up, a streak of lightning lit the sky from end to end. The horses reared in their shafts, so that the occupants were flung against each other.

"Mercy!" breathed Mrs. Winston as the Duke lost no opportunity in grasping Madelina about the waist.

"Thank you," she said, drawing quickly away.

Within seconds more thunder grumbled overheard and the window was lashed by sheets of rain.

The coachman whipped the horses, but they were nervous and the carriage made slow progress.

Half a mile further on, another bolt of lightning so frightened them that they jumped forward.

One of the carriage wheels hit a stone and cracked, leaving the vehicle at an unwieldy list. It could not in this condition continue its journey and the driver leapt down to explain the situation.

"You must take a horse out of the shafts and go for help," screamed the Duke.

The driver was struggling to follow these orders when a rider appeared out of the pouring rain.

It was Oliver de Burge, returning from his visit to Villers Court.

Taking in the situation at a glance, he took instant command. The Duke and Mrs. Winston were told to take a horse each to ride home, while the driver must remain with the carriage until help was sent from Belmont.

"And Madelina?" asked Mrs. Winston suspiciously.

De Burge looked her straight in the eye.

"Madelina will ride front saddle with me," he said.

Mrs. Winston would have liked to protest, but it was obvious that her own bulk and the Duke's meant that they could neither of them share a horse with Madelina.

De Burge's plan was agreed. The Duke and Mrs. Winston hoisted themselves onto the carriage horses, while de Burge dismounted to lift Madelina astride Solomon's back. There was no question of propriety as side-saddle would not be safe in such weather.

The trio set out, de Burge holding Madelina about the waist. She felt that his grip was strangely tender, as if he feared that he might crush her frame.

Shivering, she turned her face into his chest to hide from the rain. He said not a single word to his charge, but the sound of his breath in her ear spoke volumes.

*

Beth whispered to Madelina that Mr. de Burge had promised the Duke that he would join the company for tea after the ladies had changed out of their damp clothes.

Madelina gave a smile at the thought and then she looked across to where her stepmother sat by the fire.

Mrs. Winston was in a cross mood. She was not a natural horsewoman and her whole body ached.

She would have liked to take to her bed, but dared not leave Madelina unsupervised with that dreadful Oliver de Burge lurking about. Heaven would only know what had passed between the two of them on the way back.

Rising stiffly as Madelina watched, she hobbled to the door.

"I will see you below," she said. "Please don't keep myself and the Duke waiting."

Madelina was at the mirror, humming under her breath while Beth buttoned her gown at the back.

She could still feel the pressure of de Burge's hand under her ribs. So very close to her heart, she told herself, blushing at the thought. And had he been able to feel its fevered beat under his fingers?

On the silent ride home, some unspoken bond had formed between the two of them.

The rain had lashed at their bodies, the strong wind had torn at their clothes, but de Burge's firm hold on her had never faltered.

As she pressed closer and even closer to his manly chest, she could have sworn that she heard him murmur her name.

Soon they seemed to meld into each other, to be as one under the weather's assault. She could not be sure if it was the wind or de Burge's breath that stirred the hair at her temples and if it was the rain or his lips that brushed the nape of her neck.

Despite the cold, she was so hot, her blood pulsing feverishly in her veins.

She could not name the feelings that surged through her. All she knew was that she yearned, craved and silently begged to be kissed by this handsome strong deliverer.

She would not have cared if the ride had lasted till midnight. Indeed, as their mount clattered into the stable yard, she felt her heart sinking at the thought of being rent from de Burge's arms.

It seemed that he shared her sentiments, for when Solomon reared to a halt, he did not at once dismount. He stayed on, his arm still tight around her, the two of them listening to the stallion's breath and the rain on the cobbles.

It was only when a stable boy ran out with a cape for the horse that he stirred.

"Come, lady," he said. "We are at Belmont."

He leapt down and held out his arms. She slid from the stallion, the hem of her damp petticoat catching on the saddle so that he had to reach behind her to loosen it.

As he straightened, their eyes met and held.

She saw his pupils flare, his jaw clench as if he was labouring under some supreme effort of self-mastery.

Her face was lifted up to his and his hand in the small of her back held her steady.

The stable boy had hung a lantern on a hook when he emerged with the cape for Solomon.

In its flickering light de Burge's gaze burned into Madelina. He bent his head so that his face was no more than a hand's breadth from hers.

Madelina's eyes moved to his mouth and she gave a shudder. She half-rose on tiptoe, felt his lips brush hers so lightly that she could not swear if it was a kiss at all.

Then the stable boy gave a shrill whistle and loudly patted Solomon's rump.

As if returned by this to his senses, de Burge passed his free hand across his brow and stepped back.

"You must get out of those wet clothes," he urged.

Released from his grip, Madelina felt bereft, ejected from some haven. She began to shake as she suddenly felt strands of wet hair plastered to her cheeks and her soaking skirt where it clung to her body.

De Burge's expression changed.

In an instant he was full of concern. Cursing his own folly under his breath, he scooped her up in his arms and carried her quickly into the house.

Servants stared askance as he hurried up the stairs and, reaching an arm from under his burden, hammered on Madelina's bedroom door.

It opened and Beth peered anxiously out.

"Has Mrs. Winston returned yet?" he demanded.

"She's just stepped into her bath, sir."

This seemed to satisfy de Burge, for he thrust past her and deposited Madelina gently on the bed. He lingered for just one second, his eyes devouring her shivering form.

Then he turned and strode to the door.

"See to your Mistress," he ordered Beth and left.

Madelina's cheeks now flamed in the mirror as she recalled it. This was the effect of de Burge upon her. And what would it have been like if they had actually kissed?

She met Beth's eyes and her blush deepened.

"All done, miss," said Beth with a knowing grin.

Madelina frowned and swung away from her maid.

"I must go down. Just lay out my night things and then you may go. I shall undress myself tonight."

"Thank you, miss," smiled Beth, but Madelina was already through the door.

She moved so fast down the stairs that she caught up with her stepmother outside the drawing room.

The Duke and de Burge rose as the ladies entered. The gentlemen had changed as well and de Burge looked particularly elegant in a muslin shirt and velvet waistcoat.

He gave Madelina a short bow, but seemed to be unwilling to meet her gaze, which made her feel suddenly uncertain after the closeness of their ride home together.

She glanced at her stepmother, who had advanced to commandeer the sofa.

"I must thank you for bringing me back – so safely, sir," she then said in a low voice to de Burge.

This forced him to then stare at her and it seemed to unsettle him. But then she was not to know that she was looking particularly fetching.

Her colour was high from the warm bath she had just taken and her skin was glowing and moist. Her hair was loose since it was still too damp to arrange.

Wearing low felt slippers and with a green shawl thrown hastily about her slender frame, she had an air of considerable vulnerability and innocence about her, an air that most gentlemen would find hard to resist.

But de Burge seemed perversely determined to do just that.

"My duty, madam," he said coolly and turned aside.

Feeling as if scorched by the fire, Madelina sank onto the sofa and stared in utter dejection at the carpet. He might as well have hit her, so unexpected was his response.

Mrs. Winston as usual had seen all.

'The devil!' she thought with indignation. 'Trying to arouse the poor girl's interest by withholding his.'

She wondered what topic he and the Duke had been discussing before they arrived.

In fact the Duke had been confessing to de Burge his overwhelming regard for Madelina. She was a little bit skittish, he thought, but her stepmother had assured him that she was keen to be a Duchess.

"I will tell you, de Burge, I'll rope that filly or my name's not Tunney," he had boasted.

De Burge had said nothing, but the Duke's prior claim to the girl and his assertion that she was interested in his title was much on his mind when Madelina and Mrs. Winston entered the room.

Despite his affected indifference, de Burge's eyes roved her way all during tea. When at one point the shawl slipped from her shoulders, he seemed to be dazzled by the porcelain gleam of her skin in the firelight.

When she turned towards the hearth, he noted her ethereal paleness and only once did she catch his regard.

De Burge could not disguise an intake of breath and the Duke glanced up at the sound.

"Move away from the heat, there, Cousin, if it's smothering you," he advised.

"Thank you, I will," he replied and crossed to the window, where he stood staring out at the gathering dusk.

Mrs. Winston followed him with narrowed eyes.

"I believe you mentioned a party, Duke," she said.

"I've not forgotten," cried the Duke. "It was on my mind just now. I will send out the invitations tomorrow morning. Earl Villers will come and the Montmorencys and Sir Harry Pocklington. I'll hire some musicians and we'll have a dance. That'll please Miss Madelina, I hope?"

He was passing a plate bearing a large meringue to Madelina and she took it without a word.

It was Mrs. Winston who answered for her, turning her attention from de Burge to do so.

"Oh, Madelina adores to dance, Duke. Be sure to mark her dance card early, lest some less scrupulous fellow attempts to claim her."

With some satisfaction she sensed de Burge shift at the window under the intended barb.

The Duke chortled.

"I will, I will. I like to dance myself, you know."

Madelina was listening with lowered head. Unless de Burge showed some interest in her, she was interested in nothing. She berated herself for this pitiful state of mind, but could not change it.

She lacked the sophistication to play games with any gentleman, let alone the object of her desire.

She could not account for the abrupt change in his behaviour. Unless – it was the mention of Earl Villers!

Had this pricked de Burge's conscience because he had an understanding with the Earl's daughter, Lady Kitty?

At the thought Madelina's heart seemed to plunge like a stone down a deep, deep well. There was no end to the sickening fall.

If there was a dance and the Earl attended, then so no doubt would Lady Kitty.

All thought of the tall woman in the fox fur had vanished from her mind on that long ride this afternoon.

And there had been no one in the world but Oliver de Burge and she could have sworn that there was no one in the world for him but her.

Now she wondered. The words of her stepmother rose in her mind just like bubbles, 'a man about town' and 'whispers sweet nothings to any girl who takes his fancy'.

De Burge had decidedly not whispered any 'sweet nothings' to her when he held her on Solomon. But he had spoken with his eyes when they had both alighted in the yard and perhaps his eyes had whispered 'sweet nothings'.

Perhaps she, the foolish little American girl from Albany, had mistaken the significance. She had definitely thought that burning look to be sincere.

"Aren't you going to eat that meringue?" she heard her stepmother ask. "The Duke chose it specially for you."

Madelina raised it to her lips and then put it down.

"I am just not hungry, Stepmama," she confessed.

"Oh well, waste not, want not!" said Mrs. Winston, taking up the meringue. "I'm sure the Duke won't mind."

Looking up, Madelina was then mortified to see de Burge watching Mrs. Winston with derision.

She was indeed fond of her stepmother and hated to see her make a fool of herself and so she gently retrieved the meringue from her.

"Stop your teasing, Stepmama."

Mrs. Winston, sensing that she had overstepped the mark in such grand company, knew enough to play along.

"Madelina will always find me out," she explained with an uneasy giggle. "I try any little trick to get her to eat. She's just too thin for my liking."

"Not for mine!" came in the Duke at once. "She's just perfect as she is. Eh, de Burge?"

"Indeed," was all he could say, his voice cold.

"She'll be the belle of the ball," mused the Duke. "Won't be a female there to match her. Begad, the Earl's daughter herself will have a run for her money, eh?"

"Lady Kitty would think it beyond her dignity to have to run for anything," pointed out de Burge.

It might have been a mild criticism of Lady Kitty, but Madelina did not think so. He was now defending her because he cared for her, there was no doubt about it. No doubt he was as ambitious to marry into a titled family as her own stepmother.

How could she ever have thought that he might be attracted to her, a rich but untitled and unsophisticated girl from a small town on the East Coast of America?

De Burge was ambitious and greedy and loathsome, just loathsome! But, even as she said the words to herself, her heart rebelled, as her lips felt again that soft brush of his lips and her ribs felt the imprint of his strong hand.

And she sensed that she was lost.

Lost to love, in a way that she had never dreamed of and she would never have wished for!

CHAPTER FOUR

The Duke was so excited at the thought of his party that he retired to his study to compile a list of guests.

Mrs. Winston decided to take a nap before dinner, although it was rather late in the day to do so.

De Burge did not announce his intentions, but Mrs. Winston was determined to give him no chance to savour Madelina's company alone.

So she demanded that Madelina also retire.

"No doubt we will be seeing you at dinner," Mrs. Winston remarked frostily to de Burge.

"No doubt," de Burge replied, equally frosty.

It had become torture now to be in his presence, yet Madelina cast a longing look his way. Darkness had fallen and she could not help but admire the noble shape of his head in the moonlight from the window.

Entranced, she was unaware of the Duke at her side until she felt her hand grasped and raised to his lips.

Just in time she suppressed a gasp of distaste.

"Oh – D-Duke!" she stammered.

"Just bidding you adieu until dinner," he grinned.

Aware that Mrs Winston looked on with pleasure, the Duke turned over Madelina's hand to kiss her palm.

This was a step too far and so, forgetting herself, Madelina snatched her hand away with a wince.

The Duke straightened with a frown, perplexed by her unenthusiastic response to his attentions.

Meanwhile a stir from the window suggested that de Burge had registered the incident with some interest.

Mrs. Winston gave a studied anxious laugh.

"Dear Duke, the girl is not really herself, she is so exhausted with the ride this afternoon."

"Of course, of course," muttered the Duke.

"I am not tired at all," frowned Madelina, but her protest was ignored as Mrs. Winston caught hold of her elbow and drew her towards the door.

"*A bien toot!*" that redoubtable lady trilled, before steering her stepdaughter out into the corridor.

"What on earth were you thinking of, pulling your hand away from the Duke like that?" she hissed.

Madelina cast about for an excuse that would not entirely alienate her stepmother.

"His moustache was wet," she said at last.

"As if that mattered!" cried Mrs. Winston, but she said no more.

She must not on any account so belabour Madelina that she became suspicious of her intent.

Once in her bedroom, Madelina lay down to rest, but her eyes sprang open at every sound. It was as if her feelings for de Burge had honed her senses to be more alert than usual.

At last she sat up and, arms curled about her knees, stared at the glowing embers in the grate. They seemed to flare like rubies in the ash.

The world was becoming so bright and so intense and all because she cared for a man she should despise.

She was ashamed that he had witnessed the recent exchange with the Duke. What had he been thinking of to kiss her palm like that?

Madelina then reached for the book that sat by her bedside before realising that she had finished it last night.

It was the last of her books, but she had no wish to borrow one from Mrs. Winston whose taste ran to religious tracts she did not understood but made her feel virtuous.

The only place to find a book now was the library, which reflected the taste not of the Duke himself but the tastes of his distinguished forebears. Surely she would find something to read there?

The library seemed empty, although a fire crackled in the hearth and there were two oil lamps.

It was difficult to see the titles in this low light, so Madelina took up a lamp and used it to scan the shelves.

"I would recommend *The Lays of Ancient Rome*," came a dry voice from the shadows.

Madelina swung round at once.

In a wing-back chair by the fire sat de Burge, one leg thrown over his thigh and a glass of brandy in his hand. His shirt was loose and his waistcoat was unbuttoned.

His eyes gleamed as he surveyed her. She stood trembling in the rays of the lamp, which seemed to send a rosy ripple across her face.

She had come down without a shawl and her gown, although not cut low, revealed just enough to make her feel suddenly naked.

"Mr. de Burge! I did not expect to find you here."

He raised his drink to his lips.

"I had not expected to find *you* here," he countered, before draining the glass.

All this while he had not taken his eyes from her, as she remained transfixed, her cheeks burning and her bosom heaving. To be so utterly under his gaze seemed to drain her of the capacity to move or speak.

And if only she was able to decipher his expression and understand what that curl of the lip meant or what the flare of those nostrils signified.

"Would you care to sit down?" he asked at last in a slightly mocking tone. "Or am I not distinguished enough company for you?"

Now Madelina hesitated. She lowered the lamp she was holding and moved towards another wing-chair.

She sat down, eyes lowered. For a moment silence reigned, broken only by the crackle of the fire.

Then another sound made Madelina rear her head. Still gazing at her, he was unthinkingly rapping his finger against the rim of his glass.

Their eyes met and locked together.

She was shocked by the charge that seemed to fly from his being. His eyes widened, his breath grew heavy and his jaw tensed.

Madelina stared at him, her heart pounding.

Could any gaze convey so much apparent torture? For that is what she sensed lay behind his strained features. She was puzzling about it when a loud crack rent the air.

De Burge cursed under his breath and she saw to her horror that his glass was shattered in his fist.

She started up with a cry as a drop of blood and then another oozed from his palm.

"You are bleeding, sir."

With his other hand he waved her concern away.

"It's no great matter," he muttered.

But Madelina darted instinctively forward, drawing out a handkerchief that she kept in her sleeve.

Kneeling before him she carefully opened his hand and removed the remnants of the glass from him and then dabbed at his cuts with the handkerchief.

He made not a sound, but when she looked up, she could see that his eyes had narrowed, whether with pain or suspicion at her concern she could not tell.

"I will bind my handkerchief about your hand," she murmured. "But you will need to have the wound washed and there is no water here."

Carefully she tied the handkerchief over his palm and, having done this, she half rose, but with his other hand de Burge caught hold of her wrist so tightly that she was drawn to her knees again.

"S-sir!" she protested, as his grip was hard. "You are hurting me!"

"Is it not a fair exchange," he asked roughly, "for the pain you have caused me?"

"I – cause you pain?"

Madelina was bewildered and she wondered quite how many glasses of brandy de Burge had imbibed.

"Deuce, but I am tormented!" he groaned and then angrily thrust her from him.

She fell sideways onto her hand and her hair flew over her face like a veil.

A sob rose in her throat. What was this? Was de Burge mad that he should treat her so?

"S-sir," she whispered faintly. "What have I done to deserve this?"

Brushing her hair from her face, she sat up on her heels and de Burge turned away from her gaze.

"You have done nothing," he replied huskily after a moment. "Forgive me."

The catch in his throat surprised Madelina. Feeling a sudden pity for whatever emotion was troubling him, pity even if it involved the haughty Lady Kitty, she placed a tentative hand of comfort on his knee.

The next moment he had seized it into his bound hand, flinching briefly with the pain. Raising her hand to his lips, he hesitated, turned it over and kissed her palm.

Madelina's eyes grew larger and then closed as a wave of ecstasy ran like a flood through her body.

The Duke's self-same kiss was forgotten. She felt de Burge's warm lips linger on her soft flesh and was sure that she would faint away completely.

Not for a moment did she consider the impropriety of his behaviour. She was as if under a spell, beyond the censure of her stepmother or Society at large.

De Burge withdrew his lips and she still felt their imprint on her burning palm.

Swaying on her heels, she opened her eyes in an agony of desire such as she had never experienced.

The gaze that met her was so cold and so sardonic that she could not help but give a cry of alarm.

"My kiss displeased you?" he asked.

"Oh, n-no, sir."

"But it is of less value than the kiss of a Duke?"

"I have not had enough experience of kisses," she answered miserably, "to know what value they have."

De Burge released her hand with a sneer.

"You are making up for your inexperience today!"

Madelina raised an agonised gaze to his face.

"I-I did not seek the experience – in either case," she protested.

"No? You mean you are not hand in glove with your stepmother to ensnare my poor cousin, the Duke, by drawing him on, rejecting him, then drawing him on again? It's an old ploy, but I have seen it work with strong men."

Madelina trembled with tears.

"Ensnare? No, no. I did not intend to draw him on, I did not wish – his moustache was damp – like cobwebs over my flesh – "

De Burge gave a start.

"Cobwebs?"

Madelina nodded. She felt a tear trickle down her cheek. How could he believe her capable of playing with the Duke's affections? And why was he playing with hers?

De Burge seemed to begin grappling with his better instincts for after a moment he leaned forward and with a thumb wiped away a tear from Madelina's face.

Then he sat back, his brow creased.

"You are so young," he muttered.

"I am nineteen, sir," she said with a hint of pride.

"Hmn! It is nine years since I could so boast."

Her eyes still misty, Madelina now considered him carefully. Although there was just a touch of grey at one temple, she would not have thought him to be nearly thirty.

"Then you have behaved – in a manner ill-befitting your years," she pronounced after a moment.

De Burge gave a roar of angry laughter.

"By Heaven, you are right, madam. Put it down to this, I am a man who does not like to lose self-mastery."

He looked down at her, his face clouding.

"And you, Madelina, you – "

"And I?" she prompted after a while.

De Burge frowned and then reached for the bottle of brandy at his side.

"And you should leave a man to drink in peace," he said gruffly.

Stung, Madelina struggled to her feet. He did not help her rise, but watched her with a cold smile.

"I look forward to the continuing saga," he added. "'The Ocean of Love' saga. The girls who sail in search of crowns. Or at least heraldic symbols and country estates."

Madelina moved away from him despairingly. He was determined to believe that she was a title-hunter and nothing she could say would convince him otherwise.

She had reached the door when he spoke again.

"One thing we can in the locality thank you for is that the Duke is going to throw a party. As the divine Lady Kitty would tell you, this has not happened for years."

Madelina stiffened an instant and then passed from the room, the word 'divine' ringing cruelly in her ears.

*

When the gong rang announcing dinner, Madelina begged to be excused. She could not face the prospect of sitting with de Burge knowing his low opinion of her.

That the opinion was so undeserved did not console her, for she knew that appearances were not in her favour. Even Lady Bamber had at first suspected her of setting her cap at the Duke.

Mrs. Winston was exasperated.

"Whatever is the matter with you? You aren't ill?"

Madelina, sitting by the fire, shook her head.

No, she was not ill, at least not in the sense that Mrs. Winston intended, although her mind raced and her blood pulsed and her heart pounded at the mere memory of de Burge's lips on her palm.

"What excuses am I to make to the Duke, then?" demanded Mrs. Winston angrily. "And you have already caused him to wonder at your affections."

"M-my affections?" Madelina could not believe her ears. "As for the Duke, I have no affection for him!"

Mrs. Winston frowned uneasily.

"Surely you have friendly feelings for your host?"

"Friendly, yes," agreed Madelina.

"Well." Mrs. Winston tugged her shawl around her shoulders. "That's a start. He will not be pleased if you do not attend dinner. I'm sure he wishes to discuss the party with you."

Madelina stood firm.

"I am not hungry. Indeed my stomach churns at the very thought of food."

"You are unwell, then!" Mrs. Winston decided with a certain relief and she went off to inform the Duke.

Madelina, pressing the back of her hand to her hot forehead, wondered if perhaps she might indeed be unwell. She certainly did not feel herself. She had no appetite and her mind seemed unable to think about anything other than Oliver de Burge.

Finding that her lips were now silently mouthing the name 'Oliver', Madelina blushed.

It turned out that she need not have worried about encountering de Burge at dinner for Mrs. Winston returned later with the news that he had not attended either.

"There was just myself and the Duke and very nice it was too," she burbled. "It gave us a chance to chat."

Madelina was hardly listening.

"Why was de Burge not there?" she asked.

"Oh," replied Mrs. Winston. "He has left Belmont altogether. I believe he's gone to stay at Villers Court."

Madelina turned away so that her stepmother might not notice the effect of this news on her. She could feel the blood drain from her cheeks.

Having trifled with her feelings, having accorded her attentions that she knew in her heart were improper, de Burge had then taken off to visit the 'divine' Lady Kitty.

Did he – kiss Lady Kitty's palm too? Did he turn on her that intense passionate gaze?

A sob rose in her throat and she reached clumsily for her handkerchief to disguise it as a cough.

But the handkerchief was not in her sleeve. With a rush of emotion, she remembered that she had used it to bind de Burge's cut hand.

Why he had crushed the brandy glass in his hand she could not fathom in any way.

Mrs. Winston had detected the stifled sob.

"Have you caught a chill? Is that what has kept you from dinner? Turn to me, Madelina. My Heavens!"

Madelina's stricken features when she turned to her stepmother were such that Mrs. Winston was alarmed.

"To bed with you this instant! Beth, you help Miss Madelina undress and then go to the kitchen and make up a lemon drink. Dear me! You can't be sick for the party."

"When is it to be?" asked Madelina, as Beth hurried over to undo the buttons of her gown.

"In a week's time! And I want you to rest till then so that you're in good form."

Madelina needed no more encouragement to remain secluded for the week.

Although not physically unwell, her spirits were so low as to make her seem to be in the final stages of some wasting disease.

She was now tormented with visions of de Burge arranging the fox fur around Lady Kitty or strolling at that lady's side through shaded gardens.

The Duke sent her flowers by the basketful and little titbits to tempt her appetite, even a dish of scallops in wine, calf's foot jelly and oxtail broth.

Nothing aroused her interest at all and she gave everything to Beth, who was delighted with the opportunity to savour such delicacies.

The only diversion in the entire week was a letter from Lady Bamber with news of her travels and it consoled Madelina to think that someone held her in warm esteem.

Otherwise she ate little, exercised less and by the day of the party had the pallor of a white rose languishing in the shade.

Her eyes seemed larger than ever and burned with a strange unearthly expression.

Yet all this only served to heighten her beauty and Beth stared admiringly when she saw her Mistress dressed in her gown of tea rose silk, a single row of pearls around her neck and a silver comb in her hair.

"You're fit for an Emperor, miss, so you are!" she exclaimed.

Madelina gave a wan smile and then followed her stepmother down to the hall. She could hear the murmur of arriving guests and wondered in trepidation if de Burge and Lady Kitty were already among them.

It so happened that the carriage from Villers Court was drawing up outside at that very moment.

Thus it was that the first sight that assailed her as she descended the staircase was Oliver de Burge stepping through the front door alone.

She stopped short, hand on the stair-rail to steady her. Mrs. Winston, unheeding, sailed on down to coolly greet de Burge.

He bowed to her politely, but his eyes flew over her head until they settled on Madelina's trembling form.

Madelina started at his appearance. He looked like a man who has suffered from sleepless nights. There were hollows beneath his eyes and a deep furrow on his brow.

For an instant they stood there, eyes locked, hers yearning and his unfathomable until Lady Kitty's voice cut like a blade through the spell.

"Fancy that! My fan was behind the cushion all the time. Papa found it for me."

Lady Kitty had entered the house arm in arm with a gentleman who must surely be her father, the Earl Villers.

He inclined his head to all and sundry, while Lady Kitty, following de Burge's gaze, took in at once the pale delicate creature on the stairs.

"Ah, the Duke's guest, Miss Winston, I presume?" declared Lady Kitty loudly. "Do come down that so we can become better acquainted."

Slowly, her hand still gripping the burnished stair-rail, Madelina descended the last few steps.

The blood so throbbed in her ears that she only dimly heard yet another carriage draw up beyond the door.

Reaching ground level, she gave a curtsey to Lady Kitty and the Earl. Although de Burge now stood barely three feet from her, she dared not look his way for fear that at this close quarter his effect upon her would be noticed, particularly by Mrs. Winston next to her.

Lady Kitty's cool eye appraised Madelina, whilst the Earl put his hand under her chin and tilted her face.

"What a little pearl," he pronounced approvingly.

Madelina still dared not look at de Burge, but heard him shift from one foot to the other impatiently.

"I do hope we are going to be friends," Lady Kitty was saying in an overly sweet tone.

Reaching out, she firmly took Madelina's hand and drew her to the drawing room where guests were already mingling before the fire.

Mrs. Winston followed with de Burge on her right and Lady Kitty's little group was then announced.

The Duke broke away from other guests to greet them, paying special attention to Madelina, whom he had not seen for some days.

"Miss Madelina!" he beamed. "I am so glad that you are feeling yourself again."

De Burge gave a start at these words. He waited until the Duke signalled for drinks and then addressed her.

"You were indisposed?" he asked.

Madelina nodded, hardly able to bear his gaze.

"I-I was, sir."

"I am sorry to hear it," he said, while Mrs. Winston strained her ears to hear what was passing between them.

And Lady Kitty too was watching like a hawk.

"I daresay you will feel well enough to dance this evening?" she asked Madelina with apparent concern.

"I must confess – I always find it hard to sit still when there is music" responded Madelina.

Lady Kitty gave a short smile.

"Splendid. I am afraid that Mr. de Burge will not be free, for I lay complete claim to him, but the Duke will surely partner you and my own Papa will no doubt request one dance at least."

Lady Kitty glided on, her green taffeta skirt rustling like adders through long grass.

De Burge hesitated for a moment, then, with a brief incline of his head to Madelina, followed.

"Now there's a match made in Heaven!" observed the Duke with a chuckle.

Mrs. Winston pricked up her ears.

"A match? Is it a sealed thing, then?"

"Oh, Lady Kitty has made her mind up," answered the Duke. "And she's a girl who gets her own way. But she won't be pinned down to a date yet."

Madelina listened to this miserably. Perhaps those deep shadows under de Burge's eyes were the result of his attempt to 'pin down' Lady Kitty.

Although he had seemed concerned to hear that she, Madelina, had not been well, little knowing that he was the cause of it, yet he had not contested Lady Kitty's claim on him for the evening.

He was seemingly content to partner Lady Kitty in every dance, while she, Madelina, had to make do with the Duke and Earl Villers.

Supper was served at nine o'clock and at ten-thirty the string quartet hired for the evening struck up.

In the middle of the dance floor Madelina floated like a spectral swan on a moonlit lake. Every man in the room was interested in her, but she had eyes for none.

She moved round the room in the arms of the Duke and twice with Earl Villers without ever looking into either man's face or proffering them a smile.

'Egad,' thought the Earl after a while, 'she's a gem to look at, but cold as a carp!'

So he left Madelina solely to the Duke's attentions, who mistook her indifference for shyness.

When an interval occurred, Madelina escaped into a small chamber off the ballroom, taking with her a glass of lemonade. She stood at one of the French windows, which was ajar for air and breathed in the scent of honeysuckle.

"Would you care to dance with me?"

The voice at her shoulder was low and husky with emotion. Turning her head quickly, she met the dark and brooding stare of Oliver de Burge.

"Mr. de Burge! But – you are promised to Lady Kitty for every dance."

De Burge took no notice, but held out his hand.

"I repeat, madam. Would you care to dance?"

Madelina, despite every misgiving, gave him a nod.

De Burge gently took the glass from her hand and, encircling her waist, he drew her trembling frame to him.

She felt herself melt into his embrace and, as the music struck up in the ballroom beyond, her heart swelled in her breast. For a few blissful beats she was lost.

But then, uttering a cry, she pulled away, placing her hands on his chest to keep him at a distance.

"What is it?" he asked calmly, his face in shadow.

"I don't understand!" she exclaimed. "You believe that I am pursuing the Duke, yet you hold me in your arms. You are to marry Lady Kitty and we should not be dancing here – like this – "

She tried to release herself from his grasp, but he held firm.

"Madam, Madelina, whilst I was at Villers Court, I received a letter from France, from Lady Bamber. And its contents shamed me, for she wrote with great affection of you and professed absolute conviction of your innocence regarding any matrimonial interest in the Duke."

Though relief flooded her at these words, Madelina stood her ground.

"That does not address the matter of your interest in Lady Kitty."

"Lady Kitty!" De Burge was momentarily amused. "Her interest waxes as fast as mine wanes. An odd feature, I fear, of her singular nature."

Madelina broke free of his grip.

"Still, it does not give you the right – "

He dropped his gaze from hers. For a moment he stood, dejected. Then he passed a hand through his locks.

"If dreaming then does not give me the right," he asserted. "If longing, yearning and burning does not give me the right, what in Heaven's name does?"

Dreaming, longing, yearning, burning! The words seemed music to her ears. They were surely the words of a lover? But – was he free to address her so?

He raised his head and was now scrutinising her.

"Well?" he demanded. "Do I have the right to hold you in my arms, like any other man here this evening?"

Madelina struggled to reply and, with a gesture of impatience, he caught her hand and clasped it to his chest.

"Now do you feel my heart beating?" he demanded, almost angrily. "I am not used to feeling this way! For pity's sake, grant me this one thing. Dance with me or I'll not answer for the consequences!"

Though Madelina could not begin to imagine what these consequences might be, his expression and his voice were so serious that she dared not refuse his request.

With a sigh that was half reluctance and half desire, she slipped into his outstretched arms.

CHAPTER FIVE

It might have been an hour that passed or two or three. Or it might have been no more than five minutes.

Madelina was in another world, where time did not exist. She heard the music finish in the adjoining room, but de Burge did not release her.

They continued to circle in silence, nothing but the faint sound of their feet on the tiled floor to remind them that they were still on earth.

Her eyelids trembled and lowered with ecstasy, her eyelashes fluttered on her cheeks.

She hardly dared to breathe for fear of breaking the spell. Her heart throbbed with joy, her body ached with a desire that she could not name.

She only knew that if she could melt into his being, she would. She wanted to dance forever and she wanted to be held fast in his embrace for the rest of her life.

De Burge's hand on her waist seemed to inflame her flesh even through her gown.

He murmured her name and her eyes flew open to meet his hungry stare.

He could not settle his gaze on any one feature of her face, but devoured all in turn. Her brow, her cheeks, her eyes, her lips.

Madelina felt blood rising to the surface of her skin until she was as good as on fire.

His eyes now lingered on her lips. She turned up her face in innocent longing.

He bent his head closer, closer, and she swayed in anticipation at the thought of his passionate kiss.

A moan rose in his throat and a small cry escaped her, before lips met lips and every sound between them was sealed.

Her heart beat hard against her ribs and her body strained to join his.

This was a state beyond ecstasy. They kissed until there was no breath left in their bodies.

When de Burge drew back, Madelina stood panting in his arms. His eyes were dark with passion and he leaned towards her again, then restrained himself with a groan.

"No! I must be sure – " she heard him murmur.

Sure of what? Her pleading eyes must have asked the question, for his hands flew to grip her by the elbows.

"Sure that you are free, madam. Sure that I am not chasing a phantom."

"A – phantom?"

He groaned again.

"A spectre who haunts all my dreams and excites a desire that I dare not admit. No woman has ever held such sway in my heart."

Her own heart soared at his words. She, Madelina, to excite such desire! She, Madelina, to hold him!

It was all beyond her wildest dreams and her eyes shone as they gazed upon Oliver de Burge.

Her lips opened, a sigh fluttered from her and he was lost again.

"No man living could resist you," he cried, almost in anger.

A hand now on each of her elbows, which he forced to her side, he kissed her again, but now so roughly that the pleasure was mingled with pain.

At last she could not help but wince and he released her at once.

"I have hurt you!"

His eyes were distraught. Catching her hand, he lifted it to his lips and brushed a consoling kiss on its palm.

"Very nice, I must say!"

The voice of Mrs. Winston rang out like a gunshot in the small chamber.

Madelina broke away from de Burge with a gasp and his arms fell to his side. He cast Madelina one last impenetrable glance and then turned to face the intruder.

Mrs. Winston was boiling like a lobster in the pot.

"Do you have no shame, sir, to have secreted my stepdaughter here in this chamber and to have accosted her in this manner?"

Before de Burge could reply, Madelina, broke in with a measure of indignation.

"He did not secrete me here, Stepmama. I was here already."

"Ha! So you were waiting for him, were you? You had made an assignation?"

Madelina was about to answer again, but de Burge held up his hand to stop her.

"Madelina, let me speak," he began.

Mrs. Winston rounded on him fiercely.

"So it's 'Madelina' now, is it? Do you realise, sir, that my stepdaughter is as good as engaged?"

Madelina cried out in horror, while all the colour seemed to drain from de Burge's face.

"I think that cannot be the case, madam," he said, but without conviction.

"Not the case!" exploded Mrs. Winston. "Let me tell you, my stepdaughter is legally under my jurisdiction. The Duke has asked my permission for Madelina's hand in marriage and I have given it."

Madelina's hands flew to her mouth. She stared at her stepmother too shocked to speak.

"She may refuse," pointed out de Burge quietly.

Mrs. Winston gave a grim nod.

"Oh, she may. But remember that I have the right to withhold permission for her to marry anyone else."

Madelina at last found her tongue.

"Only t-till I am – twenty-one!"

"Long enough to prove a discouragement to anyone interested in your fortune," added Mrs. Winston sharply.

Madelina recoiled at once at the intended slight on de Burge's character, while he darkened in anger.

"I am not insensible to your meaning, madam," he said coldly.

"I don't mean you to be, sir. I am well accustomed to guarding my stepdaughter's honour, for she clearly has little enough sense to guard it herself."

Madelina opened her mouth to vigorously protest, but Mrs. Winston raised her voice to such a pitch that she was silenced before she began.

"Do you suppose, Mr. de Burge," continued Mrs. Winston, "that you are the first to attempt to ensnare her in this way? Do you think that you are the first to turn her pretty head and fill her with foolish notions?"

"Stepmama!"

Now Madelina broke out with a cry, but it was too late. De Burge had frozen at the implication inherent in

Mrs. Winston's last speech that Madelina had often fallen prey to romantic overtures from self-interested suitors.

Drawing himself up, he addressed the stepmother without a further glance at the stepdaughter,

"Please will you accept my assurance that the scene you witnessed was in no way the fault of your charge. I cannot apologise for my interest, only for my behaviour."

"Behaviour that I hope will not recur!" said Mrs. Winston firmly.

"It will not, madam."

He turned to go, but Madelina moved quickly to put a hand on his arm.

It was clear from the look he turned upon her that he struggled with his emotions, but he had no opportunity to express them, for now another voice intruded upon the air of the little chamber.

"Oliver! Where did you get to? We have missed a whole dance and a half."

It was Lady Kitty, her eyes narrow as she surveyed him standing there with Madelina and Mrs. Winston.

Madelina's hand slipped despairingly from his arm as Lady Kitty sallied further on into the chamber. She was wearing her fox fur stole.

A fox's head lolled at her shoulder and Madelina shuddered a little at the predatory expression it seemed to share with its wearer.

Lady Kitty drew up before de Burge and tapped his chest with her fan.

"Naughty man! You are promised to me for the whole evening. What do you mean by abandoning me for the company of Miss Madelina here?"

"It did not seem like abandonment when you were so deep in conversation with another," he countered stiffly.

"Oh, you mean the Duke? I was drawing him out, Oliver. He can be so secretive, but he soon revealed that he is in a position to be congratulated."

De Burge tensed.

"He is?"

"Indeed! He admitted that he and this sweet lady here are as good as engaged. There! I've let the cat out of the bag, I'm sure. But I just could not resist it. Now, shall we return to the dance floor?"

Whatever his thoughts de Burge was too much of a gentleman to do anything other than comply. He held his arm out for Lady Kitty and led her back to the ballroom.

Madelina then sank onto a gilt chair, its upholstery frayed and faded, and stared miserably at the floor.

How long ago was it she had danced in de Burge's arms, feeling that nothing could ever snatch her from him?

She had briefly tasted Heaven. Now she felt herself in Purgatory.

Mrs. Winston turned to her desolate stepdaughter,

"Aren't you going to return to the ballroom?"

"No." Madelina's reply was short.

Mrs. Winston stood for a moment, uncertain, until Madelina gave a huge sigh and spoke again,

"Why did you say that about other suitors? You know it's not true."

"Oh, but it is!" insisted Mrs. Winston. "You were always too green to see what your callers were about."

Madelina cast her mind back carefully to consider the various young men who had turned up at her home in Albany to pay their respects.

"Whatever they were about," she said at last, "I was never swept away by them, as you suggested."

"And I said that for your own good!" snapped Mrs. Winston. "You just cannot see what that Mr. de Burge is after. Your fortune dazzles him."

"And does my fortune not dazzle the Duke?" said Madelina bitterly.

Mrs. Winston looked uncomfortable.

"He is very taken with you for your own self," she replied. "And, my dear, think of what he offers! A title such as any girl would crave."

"I have never craved a title," said Madelina simply.

"More fool you!" cried Mrs. Winston. "Now, let's return to the ballroom, before the Duke himself seeks us out. It's not polite to so neglect one's host."

Upset as she was, Madelina knew that there was a measure of truth to her stepmother's words. Whatever the Duke's motives he had proved an attentive host and there was no reason to be discourteous to him.

So, disguising her reluctance, Madelina then stood up and followed her stepmother out into the ballroom.

The sudden glare of lights made her blink after the semi-shadow of the little anteroom.

She cast a longing look back at it. It was very like a chamber in her heart, where many dreams of happiness prevailed.

And his sublime kisses!

For a brief moment she had dwelt in that enchanted space where Love is the supreme law. Love! She seemed to taste the very word on her tongue.

Her longing evoked by romantic novels read before the fire in Albany, now seemed exposed for what they were – childish fancies. They could not match the power of what she felt for Oliver de Burge or the pain inflicted at this latest parting from him.

She was barely aware of the Duke looming before her and did not resist when he took her onto the floor. It was as if all will had deserted her.

A faint whiff of port then assailed her nostrils as her partner breathed out to her his pleasure in her company and his delight that she would consider his suit.

When had she actually agreed to consider his suit, she wondered, but she said nothing.

She felt trapped within the web her stepmother had spun. The Duke was their host. How could she set about disabusing him of the idea that she was willing to consider his proposal?

She had been so unaware of the plot being hatched between himself and Mrs. Winston for her future life that she had perhaps not made her opposition clear.

When she had demurred at some approach, it might have been taken as the natural coyness of an inexperienced girl. Now she did not know what she should do, except to appear to 'consider' the suit until such time as she could politely decline his hand.

'It has all gone too far!' she thought, suddenly faint with dismay.

The Duke felt her seem to sink and gripped her ever more tightly about the waist.

A shudder ran through her at his touch.

How different this was to what she had felt with de Burge. With him she could well imagine yielding herself up entirely to his passion.

Every fibre of her being strained towards him, even while she accepted that this desire was now doomed. Yet she could still dream, she could still abandon herself to his image when alone in her room. As long as she was not in the embrace of another – another such as the Duke!

"Are you enjoying the party?" she heard the Duke ask, his voice seeming to her to come from a vast distance.

She forced herself to give him a mute nod.

"Capital!" cried the Duke. "Capital!"

She turned from his beaming face to see Lady Kitty and de Burge circling the floor. Her heart plunged like a bird wounded in the air down to the cold earth.

Lady Kitty's head was almost resting on de Burge's shoulder. He himself was staring resolutely ahead. It was hard to know what he felt for the woman in his arms, but easy to see that Lady Kitty felt secure.

'She will have him,' she thought in desolation.

De Burge's comment that Lady Kitty's interest in him waxed as his interest in her waned rang hollow now in Madelina's ears. She only recalled the Duke saying that here was a '*match made in Heaven*', that Kitty Villers was a girl who always '*gets her own way*'. What else – that Lady Kitty would not be '*pinned down*' yet to a date.

Gazing at Lady Kitty now, melding her body with determination into de Burge's, Madelina could not but feel that her mind had changed.

Lady Kitty looked just like a lady who had decided to 'pin down' the man of her choice – the very same man for whom Madelina herself would pine away until Eternity, if Eternity was ever granted to her fevered soul.

*

Supper was announced. In the *melée* Madelina cast round wildly for de Burge, only to see him escorting Lady Kitty to the dining hall.

He had regained his composure to such an extent that he seemed once again the haughty cool gentleman she had once admired only from a distance.

For her part Lady Kitty had abandoned the fox fur and a great diamond necklace about her neck was revealed in its full glory.

Its sparkle seemed to strike Madelina's eye with a cruel force, particularly when the Duke informed her that it had been a birthday present from Mr. de Burge.

Madelina was duly placed at the Duke's right for the meal. Mrs. Winston looked very satisfied to be seated on his left.

Lady Kitty was sitting next to Mrs. Winston, while de Burge was a little lower down the table between two large ladies with lorgnettes.

It was some consolation to Madelina that she did not have to see de Burge and Lady Kitty seated together as she had supposed. Nevertheless she was surprised that they were so parted until the Duke told her that the large ladies were great-aunts of both himself and de Burge.

"Oliver is courteous and can listen without yawning at their gossip," he explained. "I can't keep my eyes open in their company!"

That de Burge should prove an attentive nephew to two old relatives revealed another aspect of his character that Madelina looked upon him anew.

He was everything she desired a man to be and yet he could not be hers. He believed that she was promised to another, while Lady Kitty believed that he was promised to her.

Worse than that, Mrs. Winston had led de Burge to believe that Madelina was without discrimination, that she had proved herself easy prey to any suitor's attention.

Perhaps de Burge imagined that his kiss had been only one of many she had experienced!

Madelina suppressed a sob. Mrs. Winston looked at her suspiciously and suggested a sip of champagne.

Although the food was delicious, none of it tempted Madelina's appetite. She managed just two mouthfuls of each dish, which did not escape her stepmother's notice.

Mrs. Winston was soon speaking in an undertone to the Duke, while Madelina's gaze wandered down the table to where de Burge sat with his aunts.

His head was bowed patiently as they chattered, but after a moment he seemed to sense Madelina's regard for he looked up and towards her.

He seemed to register that she sat virtually alone with the Duke deeply engaged with Mrs. Winston, for his eyes flickered their way before returning to Madelina. His features revealed nothing, his eyes even less.

Their mutual stare held briefly, before he turned his attention back to his relations.

All seemed lost to Madelina. De Burge's heart had closed against her as swiftly as it had opened.

He was clearly not a man to brook loss of honour or reputation. And a feckless impressionable young girl like herself threatened both.

After dinner the ladies retreated to an upper room to fix their *toilette* before the dancing continued.

On the other side of the room Madelina noticed her stepmother and Lady Kitty sitting and talking together with their heads bowed.

Since each of them now and then cast a look at her, Madelina could not but suppose herself to be the subject of their conversation.

She was loath to return to the ballroom, but felt that she was duty bound to do so.

There was nothing for it. She must endure the sight of de Burge and Lady Kitty together. At least it was just for this evening. Then they would be gone, back to Villers Court and she would be left to nurse her wounds.

Entering the ballroom, she then saw the Duke break away from conversation with Earl Villers.

Although the Duke claimed her for the first dance after diner, the Earl approached her for the second and she was convinced that this was at the suggestion of the Duke.

The Earl held her at arms' length. She was at a loss as to what to say to him and at last asked whether he would accompany his daughter and Mr. de Burge when they left that evening or whether he had his own coach.

It was a mere conversation opener, but the effect on the Earl startled her.

"Hah, that's the point," he replied, "de Burge has decided to stay on at Belmont. Old Tunney had to agree. Family and all that. I don't like it myself. Perhaps you would persuade him not to?"

Madelina's voice caught in her throat.

"He will not return to – Villers Court tonight?"

"Not unless you see fit to persuade him otherwise," growled the Earl.

"Me?" exclaimed Madelina. "But I don't have the power to alter Mr. de Burge's plans."

The Earl stared down at her, a twist to his lips.

"I hope that is truly the case, madam. My daughter has her eye on de Burge and I have agreed to the match. As you know, your stepmother has other designs for you."

"I know," said Madelina grimly.

"Don't lose the chance of a title," admonished the Earl, "because of some romantic nonsense. De Burge is known for his roving eye. He will soon lose interest in you, and then where would you be? Besides – " Here the Earl emitted a grim chuckle. " – I would not advise anyone to cross my Kitty."

'De Burge is known for his roving eye.'

Those words so resounded in Madelina's ears that she barely digested his veiled warning about his daughter.

She had thought that de Burge was sincere in his attentions. Now it seemed he might be an accomplished seducer.

The dance ended and Madelina, with a curtsey to the Earl, made her excuses and slipped away. She went in search of her stepmother to ask whether she might now retire from the ball.

Passing through the empty hall, she was accosted by Lady Kitty, whose fox fur stole still adorned her frame.

"Madelina! Your stepmother has been looking for you. She is in the drawing room."

"Thank you," said Madelina. "I will go to her."

She was about to move on when Lady Kitty laid a gloved hand on her arm.

"You know that Mr. de Burge has decided to stay on here at Belmont?"

"So I heard."

Madelina did not look at Lady Kitty, but fixed her eyes on the drooping fox head on her breast. Its black glass eye stared mockingly back.

"And did you hear that I intend to stay with him?"

Lady Kitty's tone was sweet as molasses, but, when Madelina raised her gaze, she saw a green-eyed stare.

"I did not hear that, Lady Kitty."

"Well, now you know. I don't intend to let Mr. de Burge out of my sight. Ever!"

She moved on, her heavy scent trailing in her wake.

Madelina leaned on a tall chest that stood in the hall under a portrait of one of the Duke's ancestors.

She was shocked to have found herself warned off de Burge in this way. Lady Kitty was certainly determined to marry him.

Despite his 'roving eye' no doubt she felt herself sophisticated enough to be able to change his ways. While she, Madelina, was only a fool from across the ocean. A girl who knew nothing about English gentlemen.

Why had de Burge decided to stay at his cousin's house? Was it to toy with her before committing himself fully to the woman he intended to marry?

Was she, Madelina, a kind of rehearsal for the real thing? She could have sworn he meant what he had said to her. Even at the memory of his words her face flushed.

How could she forget him or his touch or the dark passion in his gaze? But she must.

She must.

Madelina sprang to her feet. It was clear that she and her stepmother should leave Belmont. Away from the house and its owner Mrs. Winston might cease plotting, the Duke might cease his pursuit of her and she might regain some of her equilibrium.

It was madness to remain here as prey to de Burge and a foil to Lady Kitty.

Holding up her skirt in one hand, she hurried to the stairs and started up. As she approached the top two steps a pair of gleaming boots planted themselves in her way.

Looking up, she saw Oliver de Burge, one eyebrow raised in query.

"You are leaving the ball so soon?"

Emboldened by her recent decision and armed now as she thought with more than enough information as to his character, Madelina regarded him coldly.

"I am not aware that I need your permission, sir."

De Burge winced.

"It was not so long ago that you looked upon me with more kindness."

"It was not so long ago," countered Madelina, "that I was more ignorant of your true character."

De Burge regarded her in silence for a moment.

"*Touché*," he said at last. "No doubt I deserve that. I may have made overtures that must seem rash to you."

Madelina could not suppress a breath of derision.

"Huh! I have heard of your usual manner. You are, I hear – a man about town!"

De Burge could not disguise a flicker of amusement at this. But then he grew serious again.

"It's true that I have enjoyed the company of many women. But remember I am a good deal older than you."

"Not even by ten years!" scoffed Madelina.

"Ah," said de Burge softly, "but they are the most tender years in a young man's life. Be that as it may, I have always been Master of my heart. Until – "

He did not finish, but looked away and then down at his highly polished boots and then at last at Madelina.

"Madelina," he murmured. "I have observed your stepmother and the Duke in seemingly intense conversation since our last encounter. It has occurred to me that what we have been told about each other's character may not be entirely the truth."

Madelina stared at him. Her stepmother had indeed misrepresented her character to de Burge in claiming that she was often falling under the spell of young suitors.

Perhaps Mrs. Winston and the Earl Villers too had deliberately misled Madelina as to de Burge's reputation.

He now put out his hand.

"Come, young lady. Shall we shake on a promise to reserve judgement until we know each other better?"

Timidly Madelina gave a nod and offered her hand.

De Burge grasped it at once and his fingers closed over hers and her heart leapt at his touch.

"Oliver, I find you again with Miss Winston. What charms she must have to detain you so from the dance."

Before de Burge could reply, Madelina turned and met Lady Kitty's cool gaze from the bottom of the stairs.

"I am now about to retire for the night," she found herself saying for no reason that she could think of.

Lady Kitty gave a smile.

"Then I will bid you goodnight. We look forward to seeing you at breakfast."

Madelina heard de Burge draw in his breath.

"*We*?" he repeated.

"Oh, yes," replied Lady Kitty. "Didn't Madelina tell you? I am to stay on at Belmont too."

De Burge said nothing, but with a 'goodnight' to Madelina, passed her and continued on down the stairs.

She stared after him a moment, her heart thrilling at his manly elegant form.

Then she turned and, without a backward glance, went to her room.

CHAPTER SIX

If Madelina had hoped that her last exchange with de Burge would herald a new chapter in their relations, she was to be disappointed.

Although she saw him at breakfast and dinner and encountered him in the garden or strolling through the art galleries of Belmont, she never saw him alone.

Lady Kitty was his constant companion with her own ideas about how she and he were to occupy their time.

It was clear that she was deliberately monopolising de Burge's attention to such a degree that he would have had to be downright rude to avoid her.

And it did not help that Madelina herself was never unattended. Mrs. Winston stuck like a burr to her and the Duke made himself always available.

She could not shake them off and she began to feel just like a prisoner. There was no way of leaving Belmont without seeking the Duke's permission to use the carriage and he would never agree to her going unattended.

He would insist that both he and her stepmother act as chaperones and not Beth, whose loyalties were suspect.

Since the only time that Madelina was left on her own was when Lady Kitty and de Burge were absent from Belmont, it was clear that the main intention was to keep herself and de Burge apart.

Madelina might chafe at this situation, but she grew increasingly uncertain as to how de Burge felt. He seemed the picture of equanimity, he was attentive to Lady Kitty and politeness itself to everyone else.

She wanted to know that he yearned to be with her in the way that she yearned to be with him. She wanted to know that she haunted his dreams as he haunted hers.

All thought of leaving Belmont was gone. As long as de Burge was there and for whatever reason he seemed determined to stay, then she would stay too.

The mere sight of him was an elixir to her spirits. She lived and breathed his image.

She sensed that he was waiting, but she could not be sure for what. Meanwhile she feared that every day Lady Kitty laid greater and greater claim upon him.

The one thing that she was really glad about was the fact that the Duke had not yet formally proposed to her.

This was important, because if he did, she would be forced to refuse and after that there would be no question of her remaining at Belmont.

The Duke's reticence had surprised her at first, but on reflection it seemed evident that he wanted to be sure of her sole affections.

Mrs. Winston could not hide a certain impatience at the slow progress of her plans, but Madelina suspected that her stepmother had only herself to blame.

It was obvious that she had relayed her suspicions regarding Madelina and de Burge to the Duke, otherwise he would not be proving so instrumental in keeping them apart. Or perhaps Lady Kitty or the Earl had warned him.

Whatever the truth of the matter and however great his desire to lay his hands on Madelina's fortune, it seemed that the Duke had enough *amour propre* to want to be sure that all 'romantic nonsense' about anyone else was starved from her heart.

It was no doubt an insult to have Madelina seem to enjoy the attentions of his cousin, who had no fortune and no title! He wanted her heart entire or not at all.

His manner of seducing women had always been to shower them with gifts that he could ill afford. So he now decided that this was the best way to secure Madelina's affection. It also proved Mrs. Winston's ignorance of her stepdaughter's character that she believed so too.

The campaign itself began modestly with Madelina suddenly finding that she was the daily recipient of exotic hothouse flowers.

The accompanying card always read *Your Hopeful Admirer, Duke Tunney*. She would express polite gratitude and he would kiss her hand with his moustache trembling.

Then one morning at breakfast Madelina found a ribboned box by her plate. She glanced up in consternation. Her stepmother and Lady Kitty were present, but not de Burge or the Duke.

"W-what is this?" she asked Mrs. Winston.

"What does it look like, dear. It's a gift."

"From you?"

"No! From the Duke."

Aware of Lady Kitty's cool eye upon her, Madelina pushed the box away.

"I don't want it."

"Don't be silly," Mrs. Winston remonstrated. "You don't know what it is. Open it at least."

Reluctantly, Madelina undid the ribbon and opened the box. Inside lay a ruby bracelet.

"I cannot accept it!" she gasped.

"Nonsense, of course you can!" said Mrs. Winston. "Don't you think so, Lady Kitty?"

Lady Kitty gave a knowing shrug.

"It is not the custom in this country to reject gifts from one's host."

"It – isn't?" Madelina eyed her suspiciously.

"Indeed not. If you do not wish to accept, you must simply – leave."

Madelina looked away. Just what Lady Kitty would like. Well, she would not comply. With trembling fingers she drew the bracelet onto her wrist. It looked like vivid drops of blood on her delicate skin.

Thanking the Duke later she noticed that his lips lingered rather too long over her hand.

"I do not wish further gifts," she then said to him, drawing her hand away politely. "It's not necessary."

"But a little bird has told me that it's your birthday tomorrow," the Duke protested with an air of innocence.

Madelina knew well who that 'little bird' must be.

"I had hoped not to make it common knowledge," she complained.

"And deprive us all of the pleasure of indulging you a little?" scolded the Duke. "Heartless girl!"

The 'heartless girl' could not now help but wonder where this 'penniless' Duke was finding all the money for exotic flowers and expensive bracelets.

Her curiosity was soon satisfied.

That afternoon Lady Kitty and de Burge departed early on a trip to the town and immediately Mrs. Winston's vigilance abated and Madelina was left to entertain herself.

She and Beth took a walk through the gardens and, as they passed the window of the Duke's study, a flicker of light at the corner of her eye caused her to glance in.

Mrs. Winston was sitting at the desk, counting out gold coins from a leather reticule.

Behind, a hand on her shoulder, stood the Duke. They were so occupied with the transaction in progress that neither noticed Madelina staring in.

So that was it! Her own stepmother was actually financing the Duke's courtship and with her money!

Madelina determined to put a stop to this especially when de Burge complimented her at dinner on her latest acquisition, the bracelet. It was obvious from the irony in his tone that he knew where it came from.

She would remonstrate with the Duke at the earliest possible opportunity.

Her resolution was strengthened when the very next day at breakfast she found three parcels by her place. For a moment she imagined that they were all from the Duke until she remembered that it was her birthday.

Everyone was present and they eagerly watched as she opened her parcels.

Mrs. Winston had given her blue handkerchiefs and Lady Kitty had given her a pair of yellow kid gloves.

Madelina then reached for the third parcel. The card indicated that it was from Oliver de Burge.

She hoped that no one noticed how her hands shook as she removed the ribbon and tore off the paper.

She unwrapped a beautiful leather bound book, its title was embossed in gold on the cover, *THE LAYS OF ANCIENT ROME.*

Her eyes flew to de Burge. This was the title that he had suggested to her when she had gone to the library that evening when he had first pressed her hand to his lips.

It was a signal. He had not forgotten that encounter.

For one brief moment he met her gaze and his eyes spoke volumes. Then it was as if a veil descended again. He appeared once again the detached calm observer.

Madelina was relieved that none of the parcels were from the Duke. Her relief was, however, short-lived.

Breakfast now over the party was summoned to the hall. The front door stood open and outside waited a light open gig with a fine bay gelding in its shafts.

"For you!" proclaimed the Duke proudly. "Happy Birthday, Madelina."

Madelina was utterly speechless. It was for this that Mrs. Winston had been counting out her money yesterday!

It was a gift that implied a permanent stay here at Belmont, for there was nowhere to stable a horse and gig at their London address.

"Well?" demanded the Duke.

"This is – too generous." Madelina swallowed.

"Stuff and nonsense!" rejoined the Duke. "A young lady must have her own means of transport after all."

Madelina gave a start at these last words and her eyes widened with realisation as she gazed again at the gig.

Here was her freedom! The Duke had inadvertently provided her with the means to elude both his and her stepmother's regime. She would need no permission to use her own carriage and she could call for it the moment their mutual attention was elsewhere – and escape.

With this in mind she gave a gracious curtsey.

"Thank you, Duke. I shall really enjoy driving out in such a vehicle."

"Be sure to visit St. Dunstan's when you do," came de Burge's voice quietly.

She turned at once to where he was standing with Lady Kitty and Mrs. Winston looking on.

With a quickening of her pulse she absorbed his seemingly innocent suggestion.

He did not need to elaborate for her to grasp his meaning. Should she ever manage to get away alone, she should drive to St. Dunstan's, where he would meet her.

She just wished that he looked a little more pleased for her. His brow was furrowed and she could not help but feel that this gift to her from the Duke disturbed him.

That day it was impossible to avoid Mrs. Winston's demand that Madelina take her out on a jaunt. The Duke rode behind the gig on his mare.

Madelina held the reins and was thrilled to discover that the bay responded beautifully to her touch.

She need not then worry about driving out alone.

*

It was another two days before she had the chance to do so.

The Duke had sold four of his horses, but was still anxious to obtain some ready cash. With this in mind de Burge arranged for a wealthy neighbour to come and look at some precious old manuscripts collected by one of the Duke's forebears who had an interest in such things.

Lady Kitty considered it to be too dull for words and decided to visit her father, the Earl, whom she had not seen since the night of the ball.

Since de Burge and the Duke were occupied with the neighbour, Mrs. Winston felt she might safely abandon Madelina to her own devices as she wanted to lie down.

Madelina seized her opportunity. She slipped out to the stable yard where she ordered her carriage.

The stable boy helped her into it and was about to step back when she handed him a folded letter.

"Take this to my maid, Beth," she asked in a low voice. "Tell her to convey it discreetly to Mr. de Burge once he is alone. And not a word to anyone else."

Since her admonition came with a shilling, it was not difficult for him to promise to fulfil her bidding.

Putting the letter with a wink into his apron pocket, he next caught up the reins and handed them to Madelina.

"Gee up," she called out to the bay.

The horse started up and the carriage rolled through the stable yard gates and onto the driveway.

With luck no one at Belmont would discover her absence until she was some distance away.

*

The bay trotted gaily along, lifting his hooves high.

Madelina almost hugged herself with delight. Back home in Albany she often used to drive out alone, but from the time that Mrs. Winston had devised this trip to England she had been subject to ever increasing restrictions.

It was just as if her stepmother only saw her as an investment, a painting or a fine porcelain vase, rather than a young woman.

For the first time in a long time she felt free and she was glad of her cloak as the air was sharp.

Her note to de Burge said that she had ridden out and would be at St. Dunstan's at three o'clock. She did not exactly ask him to join her there, but he would see no other reason for her giving him the information.

She did not know what she would say to him if he came. There was unfinished business between them and the kiss that they had exchanged had forged a secret bond.

She only knew that her longing to be alone with him anywhere in the world had driven her to this somewhat reckless move.

For reckless it indeed was to imply that she would be waiting for him without a chaperone in a deserted place.

St. Dunstan's! It was half-an-hour before she saw its spire above the treetops.

She drew up before the wooden Church gate and climbed out. She opened the gate and passed through.

The churchyard was deserted. A mist was rising from the damp earth and curling about the tombstones.

Madelina hurried over to the porch and pushed at the door. It creaked heavily open and then she peered in. The interior was cold, quiet and dark. A lone candle burned on a small table where red hymnals were stacked.

Tiptoeing over to a pew, she sat down and waited.

Suddenly she was aware of hoofs on the gravel path and it was only when a step rang out on the tiled floor of the aisle that she sprang up from her seat and turned.

A figure stood at the door, back to the dim daylight.

It was de Burge and she gave a little cry of relief.

"You seem surprised to see me," he said softly.

"I hoped it was you but feared it might be another."

De Burge grasped her meaning.

"You were not yet missed when I rode away. The Duke wanted to show his neighbour round the estate and I managed to absent myself."

A silence fell between them. After all her yearning to see him alone, Madelina felt suddenly embarrassed at her boldness in summoning him here.

For his part de Burge did not seem to be inclined to speak, but regarded her without expression.

"D-did the Duke manage to sell any manuscripts?" she asked after a moment.

"Two." De Burge's reply was curt.

"I am sure he was pleased."

"Are you really interested in his pleasure, then?" de Burge's voice was sharp and she drew back.

"I should rather have him pleased than otherwise."

"For pity's sake, Madelina!" he burst out. "Did you bring me here just to discuss the Duke?"

Madelina coloured.

"I thought – when you suggested this as a place to visit – you were hoping one day to meet me here."

She was almost ready to weep at the thought that his mention of St. Dunstan's had just been a mere off-hand remark. Supposing all this time that she had misread those furtive glances and supposing that he had lost all interest in her since their last encounter?

A tear started from her eye. De Burge saw it and in an instant was at her side.

"Forgive me, Madelina!"

"I don't know what to think!" she sobbed. "You said we should – get to know each other before we made a judgement upon – each other's character. Yet how can we when we are never alone together?"

"We are alone together now."

"So what good is that," wailed Madelina, "when all you do is berate me for talking about the Duke?"

"Hush, hush!"

Taking her by the hand, he sat down beside her.

Then he knelt, leaning an elbow on the arm of the pew, one hand still grasping hers. With his free hand he drew a handkerchief from his waistcoat pocket.

Madelina stared in wonder. It was her own – the one she had bound his hand with when he had crushed the wine glass in his fist in the library.

She raised her eyes to his.

"I have kept it always near my heart," he sighed.

He was so close, but she felt no urge to fall into his arms nor did he seem to want it. It was as if they were taking stock of each other.

She drank in his features, the black eyes, the high brow and the hint of grey at his temple.

He gazed back, equally mesmerised.

Then he stirred himself and dabbed her tear-stained face with the handkerchief. All the time his eyes roved her face until they lingered on her trembling mouth.

He leaned forward, hesitated and then brushed his lips to hers. It was a chaste kiss, but it opened a flood of desire in her breast that was almost unbearable.

It seemed to work the same magic upon de Burge, for he drew back with a groan and let go her hand.

"These days at Belmont have been a taste of Hell," he said huskily. "To be so near you and have to watch the Duke paw you when he could. Did you begin to welcome his attentions?"

"How could you think so?" Madelina cried.

"I don't know what I thought. I needed to watch, to wait and to be sure that you were not the flighty young creature your stepmother had described."

"Then you seemed content enough to be with Lady Kitty," accused Madelina.

De Burge gave a grim laugh.

"At one time I believed myself in love with her, but she would not have me. Then, when I lost interest in her, she began to behave as if she had accepted my proposal. I made my position clear, but I think she believed that she had only to persevere and I would relent. I let the situation drift, it did not seem to matter one way or another, since I despaired of caring for any woman. And then you came into my life – "

He could not continue but, catching her hand again, he pressed it to his face.

"Oh, my darling Madelina," he moaned. "You have brought my heart to heel. I have watched the Duke shower you with gifts in terror that you would succumb to him."

"Never!" insisted Madelina fiercely.

De Burge gave a deep sigh.

"Then, divine angel of my heart, will you defy your stepmother to be mine?"

For her answer Madelina sank against his chest.

"I would defy anyone – to be with you," she sighed. "Sweetheart!"

De Burge said no more, but held her to him for a moment.

Then he rose, bringing her with him after secreting her handkerchief away again in his waistcoat,

He took her by the arm and led her out from the Church and helped her into the gig.

She picked up the reins and set off, her mind in a daze. Now and then she glanced at de Burge, who rode alongside on Solomon, but although he smiled at her once or twice, he seemed somewhat preoccupied.

She did not care as she was sure that he was making plans for their future.

It was growing dark as they reached Belmont.

An unfamiliar carriage sat in the driveway, a trunk roped to its back.

Looking suddenly troubled de Burge dismounted.

He was just handing Madelina down when the door opened and two servants came out to unload the trunk.

Lady Kitty appeared on the steps behind them. Still in her riding skirt, it was obvious that she had just returned from her visit to Villers Court.

She regarded Madelina and de Burge without any emotion.

"Oliver, you have a visitor," she announced.

"I recognise the carriage. My mother!"

Lady Kitty gave a cool smile.

"That's right, Oliver dear. I wrote to invite her."

He stared at Lady Kitty in astonishment.

"It might have been better to consult me first on the matter," he commented at last. "Where is she now?"

"Ensconced with Mrs. Winston. They are having such an interesting conversation. I think they are anxious for you to join them."

De Burge turned to Madelina.

"I will come to you later," he said in an undertone.

Madelina nodded and watched as he ran on up the steps into the house. Lady Kitty gave her a long appraising look and then turned and followed.

Madelina stood alone for a while and then she too went into the house.

Lady Kitty had vanished and the hall was silent, so Madelina made her way to her room, where she questioned Beth about Mrs. de Burge.

"She arrived about an hour ago, miss," Beth began, "and straightaway sent for your stepmother. They've been talkin' in the library ever since. The Duke is with them. I've heard the mother and son don't get along too well," she added, helping Madelina off with her cloak.

Beth's words felt ominous to Madelina.

Why had Lady Kitty invited Mrs. de Burge to come to Belmont if that lady and her son did not get on? And why had Mrs. de Burge upon her arrival sent straight for Mrs. Winston, a lady she had never previously met?

Madelina knew that she must wait for the answers to her questions.

After Beth had helped her into an evening gown, she sent the maid away and went to the window with the book de Burge had given her, *The Lays of Ancient Rome.*

But she could not concentrate. She longed to hear the dinner gong sound, for it would mean that she could go down and see this Mrs. de Burge for herself, as well as see Oliver again.

Oliver! Madelina closed her eyes in longing as she pronounced his name. That he longed for her was all that mattered in the world.

Leaning against the windowpane, Madelina fell into a reverie from which she was not roused until she heard the sound of a horse neighing below.

Was Mrs. de Burge leaving already? Kneeling up on the window seat, she peered out.

It was not Mrs. de Burge below, but Oliver himself. He was holding Solomon by the reins and had buried his face in the horse's neck.

Then, in a second, he grasped Solomon's mane and leapt up into the saddle. Madelina began to unaccountably tremble.

She opened the window to call out.

Too late! Oliver dug in his spurs, Solomon half-reared and they galloped wildly off into the night.

Madelina knelt there in utter disbelief. Why had Oliver taken off like that with not a backward glance and with no word sent to her?

She turned as she heard the door open.

Mrs. Winston was there, looking strangely shaken.

"W-what's going on?" asked Madelina weakly.

"What's been going on?" echoed Mrs. Winston, as if it was a question she did not wish to consider. "I'll tell you. Mr. de Burge interrupted my meeting with his mother to demand that I give your hand in marriage – to him!"

Surprised that de Burge had acted so swiftly and confused that he had then disappeared without word into the night, Madelina rose shaking from the window seat.

"And what did you reply?" she whispered.

"I didn't reply. Mrs. de Burge did."

"Mrs. de Burge? W-what did she say?"

Mrs. Winston looked most uncomfortable.

"She told her son that his suit was impossible. Not because he was promised to another or you were almost promised to the Duke, but for another reason entirely."

Madelina felt a chill invade her being.

"And what is that?"

Mrs. Winston gave an audible swallow.

"Madelina, my dear, Oliver de Burge and you share the same father. He is your brother. Your secret and long lost brother!"

CHAPTER SEVEN

A pitiful cry rose from Madelina and she then sank to the floor. She knew no more until she felt a damp cloth on her brow and two hands chaffing her own.

"Miss Madelina! Miss Madelina!"

She dimly heard a voice calling her name, but the darkness enfolding her seemed infinitely better than cruel reality that she wanted to stay there.

She fought against her returning consciousness, but nature proved the stronger. Her eyes fluttered open and at once filled with tears.

Beth knelt at her side, whilst Mrs. Winston stood anxiously behind holding a lamp.

"Oh, Madelina! What a scare you gave us!"

Madelina put a hand across her eyes to shield them from the glare of the lamp and Mrs. Winston hurried to put the lamp on a table.

"He is gone!" whispered Madelina in desolation.

"Gone!" echoed Beth. The maid bit her lip as if to continue, saw Mrs. Winston and said no more.

"Help me up, Beth," Madelina said weakly and was guided to a chair before the fire.

There she slumped to stare at the glowing coals.

"Shall I send Beth for a hot drink?" Mrs. Winston asked. "Would you like a rug over your knees?"

Madelina raised anguished eyes to her stepmother.

"I would like you – to tell me the full story about Oliv – Mr. de Burge," she said faintly.

"Wouldn't it be better, dear, to forget all about the episode?" Mrs. Winston wrung her hands.

"No!" responded Madelina fiercely. "Tell me!"

With a sigh Mrs. Winston then sat down opposite Madelina and waved Beth away. She seemed to find it hard to begin and clasped her fingers in her lap.

"I wish we'd never met Mr. de Burge!" she burst out at last. "He's been trouble to us since the beginning."

Madelina made no answer, but simply stared at her until she heaved another sigh and went on,

"It seems your father had a wife of sorts in London before he sailed to America."

Subdued as she was, Madelina gave a start.

"What do you mean by – *a wife of sorts*?"

Mrs. Winston looked embarrassed.

"As I understand, it was not a legal marriage. More of a – dalliance."

That her father should have had such a relationship in the past!

Madelina leaned her elbow on the chair's arm and covered her face with her hand as Mrs. Winston continued,

"This wife of sorts was the lady who later became Mrs. de Burge. While involved with your father, she bore him a son. Oliver."

She bore him a son.

Madelina felt chains of iron encircle her heart.

"Why did she and my father – separate?" she asked in a whisper, her hand still before her face.

Mrs. Winston's reply was itself barely audible.

"It seems he abandoned her. Knowing your father as I did, I couldn't believe it. After he had left, she quickly

97

married an old suitor, Mr. de Burge, and then moved to Shropshire. Mr. de Burge was prepared to adopt the boy and bring him up as his own, on one condition – that the child never be told of his true parentage. Mrs. de Burge agreed and your current misery is the unfortunate result."

'No wonder my father kept this liaison a secret,' thought Madelina with an inward groan. 'He would have been ashamed to admit that he had an illegitimate child, whose mother he had so coldly abandoned.'

She could never have believed it of sweet kindly Papa! But what did one ever know of another's character, even someone so close?

She took her hand from her face and asked,

"And the Duke himself had no idea?"

"No idea. He's in a state of shock too. His family connection is to Mr. de Burge, not to Mrs. So, if Mr. de Burge is not Oliver's father, then the Duke and Oliver are not blood relations at all."

Madelina turned her gaze back to the fire. She felt drained of life and of hope.

No situation she might imagine could be worse than this, that your father should by some callous action in the past have ruined your future.

That the man you loved, the man who loved you, should, because of your father, be the one man in the world you could never, never marry.

She shuddered at the memory of Oliver's kisses – illicit kisses, she now knew!

Her soul was in utter turmoil. How was it possible to know what she knew and continue to breathe or to live?

How could her shattered heart continue to beat?

"So you were present when O-Oliver was told all this tonight?" she then asked, finding it almost unbearable to pronounce de Burge's name.

"Yes." Mrs. Winston gazed unhappily at Madelina. "He listened to every word, went white as a sheet and then left without saying anything."

Madelina's thoughts returned to that view of him, head buried in Solomon's neck. He had not looked back at Belmont, but had ridden off like a man in fear of the Devil.

As well he might, for what he had felt for Madelina and what she had felt for him, was an abomination in the eyes of God and the law.

What would he do with his life now? Her soul felt as heavy as lead as she realised how clear the road ahead was for Lady Kitty to reinstate her claim on him.

She remembered that it was Lady Kitty who had invited Oliver's mother to Belmont. Why had she done it? Surely it was to engage the mother as ally in destroying the growing relationship she feared between her and de Burge.

Lady Kitty could not have suspected beforehand the bombshell in Mrs. de Burge's arsenal, for she would have used it herself long ago had she possessed it.

Lady Kitty had met herself and Oliver at the front door when they returned from St. Dunstan's. Where had she gone after that?

"Was Lady Kitty there – when Mrs. de Burge told Oliver about his – father?" she asked Mrs. Winston.

Mrs. Winston considered.

"I was alone with Mrs. de Burge when she regaled me with the lamentable story. Lady Kitty only appeared towards the end of our *tête a tête* to inform us that you and Mr. de Burge had ridden up to the house. Mrs. de Burge then asked that she straightaway fetch Mr. de Burge to the library. Lady Kitty went away to do just that. He came in soon after and Lady Kitty followed within a few minutes. So yes, she was there when Mr. de Burge heard the story."

A great bitterness seized Madelina's spirit as she thought of how great a coup this revelation of Oliver's true parenthood must have seemed to Lady Kitty.

"And no doubt she was pleasantly surprised," she remarked acidly.

Mrs. Winston glanced at her with concern.

"Pleasantly surprised? My dear Madelina, that is so ungracious of you. Though now I come to think of it – "

Mrs. Winston's voice trailed away as she cast her mind back to the unhappy scene in the library.

"Well?" prompted Madelina, her curiosity aroused.

"Now I think of it," Mrs. Winston went on slowly, "it was strange that she did not look surprised at all."

"As if she already knew!" exclaimed Madelina.

Mrs. Winston nodded.

"Exactly. As if she already knew."

The two of them fell silent, each lost in her own thoughts. Madelina wondered how long Lady Kitty had known and surmised that it could only have been since corresponding with Mrs. de Burge. She would otherwise have used the information to her own advantage earlier, as Madelina had already worked out.

Mrs. Winston was speculating about Lady Kitty's complicity in the whole matter.

In truth she had to commend Lady Kitty's strategy in bringing Mrs. de Burge to Belmont, whatever she might have known in advance. It had done the trick nicely. Mrs. Winston herself could never have devised such a plot.

Now there was nothing to prevent a match between Madelina and the Duke, except for the time it would take for the poor girl's heart to heal.

There was no doubt that she was most cut up about it all! Mrs. Winston was sorry for that. But it too might work to the advantage of her crafty plan.

Madelina's unhappiness might make her turn to the Duke's arms for comfort.

Beth reappeared with hot milk for the two ladies and they drank in silence, then Mrs. Winston, after asking if Madelina felt a little more like her old self, decided to dress for dinner.

She swept from the room, ordering Beth to follow and help her with her *toilette.*

When Mrs. Winston was out of earshot, she crossed to Madelina, who looked up and suddenly burst into sobs before her maid could say a word of comfort.

"Oh, Beth, Beth. That he should go like that – so wounded by what he had learned – without a word to me!"

"Not quite without a word, miss," whispered Beth. "Here, dry your tears."

Beth then drew a handkerchief from her bosom and thrust it at Madelina.

Madelina took it unthinkingly, went to pat her eyes and then gasped. Here it was again! The handkerchief she had used to bandage de Burge's hand.

He had handed back to her a memento of their brief and painful love.

"Unfold it, miss," Beth urged, throwing a quick and anxious glance at the door.

Madelina stared at the maid and then obeyed.

Spreading the kerchief out on her lap, she gave a start. Something was written on it!

"*FORGET ME,*" it read. "*FORGET US.*"

Madelina let out a single desolate wail. These were not words to give comfort to her stricken heart. Taking up the handkerchief, she balled it in her fist.

"Forget – forget – " she repeated, rocking herself to and fro on her chair. "That is all he can say. That is all we can do."

"Quiet, miss," urged Beth. "I don't think that Mrs. Winston would like to know that he had even sent you this. She said that other lady, his mother, agreed that they'd call the authorities if he so much as said goodbye to you."

Madelina looked at Beth miserably.

"So he is to be hounded too for his pains. How did he get this to you?"

"He sent a message through the boy who saddles up his horse that I was to wait by the front door. He gave it to me quickly before anyone could see."

"And then he left."

"Yes, miss. Lady Kitty came to bid him goodbye, but he says nothin' to her."

Mrs. Winston's voice calling from the other room roused Beth, who hurried off.

Madelina had no desire to meet Mrs. de Burge and refused to attend dinner.

She was not fooled by a note sent from Lady Kitty enquiring after her well-being. She could not quite regret Lady Kitty's action as it had at least prevented herself and de Burge from embarking on a terrifying path together.

But the malice behind her intent was unforgivable.

Mrs. Winston did later divulge that Mrs. de Burge would have been against a match between Madelina and Oliver on any ground, for she was as ambitious that her son marry into a titled family such as Lady Kitty's just as Mrs. Winston was ambitious for Madelina to marry a Duke.

Madelina heard all this almost without interest. She still refused to meet with Mrs. de Burge and, until that lady departed three days later, she would not leave her room.

The Duke, maybe at Mrs. Winston's advice, did not attempt to see her or make contact.

Beth brought her tempting meals from the kitchen, but Madelina hardly touched a thing.

She was numb, body and soul. The one image, the one name that once would have brought her some comfort, she had to resolutely banish from her mind.

Whether *he* allowed himself to think of her, she had no way of knowing.

*

On the day that Mrs. de Burge left Belmont, Beth smuggled in a letter to Madelina.

"The envelope was addressed to me, miss, but this other envelope be inside, marked for you."

Madelina opened it quickly and read the contents with trembling hands,

"*I cannot call you beloved, although you remain in my heart. I had to leave Belmont without seeing you, but not because of your stepmother and my mother.*

Their cruel commands alone would not have kept me from you, but had I set eyes on you, I could not have left at all.

We must never meet again, Madelina, unless what we felt for each other is ripped entirely from our hearts.

Until that most unlikely moment, Adieu!"

*

A long sorrowful week passed by with the weather turning decidedly colder. There was a severe frost at night and the windows in the morning were engraved with ice.

For hours Madelina traced the delicate designs with her finger until the pale winter sun finally melted them.

She then fell to pacing her room. From one corner to another, from the window to the passage door, her tiny slippered feet were on the go. All the time she fought the memory of Oliver de Burge, but she might just as well have fought not to breathe.

The effort to forget seemed to take every ounce of her energy. She ate barely enough to sustain life.

She slept only four or five hours a night for, when she slept, she dreamed and when she dreamed, it was of the very man she sought to erase from her mind and heart. So sleep became an enemy.

Lack of sleep and fresh air and little nourishment soon took their toll on her health. Her heart beat far too quickly, her hands trembled and her forehead was always moist with fever.

At last Mrs. Winston convinced her to come down to the drawing room and see the Duke.

He was frankly shocked at her appearance with the dark rings under her eyes and her skin as transparent as a moth's wing.

He plied her with delicacies and felt some sense of triumph when she accepted a dish of pears in syrup.

But she did not finish it and, excusing herself soon after, retired again to her room.

"Dash it!" he then exclaimed to Mrs. Winston as the door closed behind her. "You warned me that she and my cousin, de Burge, were in danger of being a little too taken with each other, but she's acting as if the fellow got as far as making love to her!"

Mrs. Winston did not look at him as she replied,

"Oh, no, it's nothing like that! It's just – imagine the shock! She thought that she hardly had a relative in the world. And now it turns out she has two!"

"Two?" The Duke looked surprised for a moment. "Who's the other one?"

"Why, Lady Bamber!" said Mrs. Winston.

The Duke grunted.

"Oh, yes, yes. I'd forgotten. Still I can't see why discovering she has more family than she thought should turn the girl into a husk!"

"But, Duke, just imagine learning that your father behaved in such a dastardly way," said Mrs. Winston.

The Duke threw her a look.

"Or your husband!"

Mrs. Winston lowered her head. The Duke need not have reminded her. She had found it greatly disturbing to learn that the late Mr. Winston had not been quite the man she thought.

The Duke stretched out his bulk in his armchair.

"If the girl doesn't improve," he said, "you should take her up to London to see Professor Hartford. He's a renowned specialist in nervous disorders."

Mrs. Winston was rather surprised, wondering how the Duke knew about Professor Hartford.

As if reading her mind, the Duke continued.

"He was a friend of my father's at Rugby School. Sees a great many Society ladies, I'm told."

"I'm grateful for your concern," said Mrs. Winston sincerely.

"Can't be doing with a girl wasting away under my nose."

Mrs. Winston stiffened. She had always known that the Duke's main interest in Madelina was pecuniary, but he now seemed to genuinely appreciate her personal charms.

It was clear that this appreciation was literally skin deep and his eye would wander if she lost her looks. And Heaven knows that there were many other eager American mothers out there seeking English titles for their daughters.

The Duke would soon be snapped up if she did not secure him for Madelina.

It was for this reason more than any other that she decided to take the Duke's advice on Professor Hartford.

She wrote to the Professor that very afternoon for an appointment and a reply came by return of post. The Professor would be pleased to see her and her stepdaughter in four days' time at his clinic in Harley Street.

Madelina said nothing when Mrs. Winston told her that they were to leave Belmont. Neither did she seem to care that she was to be taken to see a doctor.

She knew that what ailed her could not be cured, but if her stepmother wanted to try, so what did it matter? And besides, there was comfort in going back to London.

Lady Bamber would be there very soon as she had written to say that she would be arriving back in England too late to have Christmas at her Gloucestershire home, as she had originally planned, but hoped Madelina and Mrs. Winston would visit her in London over the Season.

Madelina had made no mention in her reply of what had passed between herself and Oliver be Burge.

It was probably wrong to keep from Lady Bamber the momentous news that she had another relation besides Madelina in the world.

But Madelina instinctively knew that Oliver would not wish what he had learned about his true parentage to become public knowledge.

Anyway no gentleman would want it divulged that he was the illegitimate child of a cad who had abandoned him and his mother for a new life in America?

She just knew that for her own sake Oliver would not wish the name of the late Mr. Winston to be publicly besmirched.

All in all, silence on the subject was best. Only a few people would know the truth, Oliver, his mother, Mrs. de Burge, Mrs. Winston, Beth and Madelina herself. Oh, and Lady Kitty Villers.

Madelina winced as she recalled Lady Kitty and her role in all this. What a torment to know that that lady would always share the terrible secret that had driven her and de Burge apart.

She could be sure of one thing, though, that Lady Kitty would kept that secret, for it would be of no benefit to her to have it known that the man she pursued had been born out of wedlock.

*

Snow threatened on the morning Madelina and her stepmother left Belmont. The cold clear air gave a little colour to her cheeks and she looked altogether healthier than of late.

The Duke looked approving and Mrs. Winston was pleased to see that he showed genuine regret at seeing them go. He promised to visit them at their house in London at the first opportunity.

As it turned out, Madelina did not go immediately to the house in Wigmore Street as Professor Hartford was so concerned about her health after examining her that he convinced Mrs. Winston to leave her in his care.

"She is suffering from morbid depression," he said. "I have seen these cases before. The decline can be quite rapid and even lead to death."

"Death!" Mrs. Winston's hand flew to her breast. "Oh, you must help her, Professor."

The Professor promised that seclusion in a place unconnected with the events that had caused the depression in the first place would soon have a positive effect.

And he would not even allow Beth to remain with Madelina, since the maid's presence would surely remind her Mistress of the past and Mrs. Winston herself must not write or visit for the first few weeks.

The clinic was in a tall elegant house and, as soon as Madelina was ensconced there, snow began to fall.

The soft flakes muffled all sounds of the City. She felt that she was now in a cocoon and Professor Hartford's therapy contributed to that sensation.

He was a kindly man with great white whiskers and a fatherly demeanour.

She meekly took all his medicinal remedies without resistance. These were herbal teas to help her sleep, iron to give her strength and St. John's Wort to lift her mood.

The Professor's wife was a cheerful bustling soul, who gradually reawakened Madelina's appetite.

Slowly the peace and quiet and the absence of any reminder of the past and the discreet care of the Professor and his wife produced a change for the better in Madelina.

She did not forget Oliver, but his image was not with her at every moment of the day. The pain was still there, but muted, a dull ache at the bottom of her heart.

The Christmas Season was fast approaching when at last the Professor felt confident enough of Madelina's recovery to allow her to receive visitors.

The first to arrive was Mrs. Winston, who had spent the last weeks in great inner turmoil. It was not within that lady's nature to blame herself for anything, but she was not insensitive to the fact that her plotting had contributed to Madelina's decline.

Had she not taken the girl to Belmont, this liaison with de Burge would never have occurred. She had indeed been too hasty in pursuing the Duke for her stepdaughter.

She was therefore simply delighted to see Made.ᴸ looking her old self.

She immediately forgot her self-recriminations and determined to renew her efforts to forge a marriage alliance with Duke Tunney.

She failed to notice that the sparkle had gone from her stepdaughter's eyes and the bright note from her voice.

"You will, of course, come home for Christmas?"

"Home?" Madelina wrinkled her brow.

"I mean to the house in Wigmore Street. Where did you suppose I meant?"

"I thought – perhaps – Albany." Madelina sighed.

"Albany!" Mrs. Winston shrieked. "You can't want to return there, surely? Now you've seen all that England has to offer?"

Madelina regarded her stepmother mildly.

"If you wish to remain here, Stepmama, I do too."

Mrs. Winston relaxed. She had not the sensitivity to realise that Madelina's agreement did not indicate affection for her, but indifference as to where in the world she was.

Madelina's body was healed, her mental health was restored, but her heart was forever broken.

The Duke was the next one to call to see her. He brought Christmas roses and hand-made chocolates. His devotion had been re-stoked by her absence and this sight of her looking so beautiful and healthy awakened in him all his old fervour and he determined once again that she and her fortune should be his.

Madelina left the clinic just before Christmas and Beth and Mrs. Winston had endeavoured to make Wigmore Street as welcoming as possible.

Madelina was quickly settled on the sofa before a roaring fire in the drawing room, a rug over her knees.

Mrs. Winston left to arrange tea and suggested that
she look at the latest magazines.

In a desultory fashion she took up one and began
to leaf through it only to have her attention arrested by an
announcement on *The Court Circular* page.

It declared the engagement of Lady Kitty Villers
and Mr. Oliver de Burge.

With a strangled cry, Madelina threw the magazine
aside. Tears quickly flooded her eyes and spilled onto her
cheeks, but then as quickly she wiped them away.

In a trice all trace of emotion was gone. Her weeks
with Professor Hartford had strengthened her resolve to
fight despair whenever it reared its head.

When Mrs. Winston returned to the drawing room,
she did not notice anything that had disturbed her.

Madelina sipped her tea quietly, her eyes glued to
the fire. She did not even start when the doorbell clanged
in the hall.

Mrs. Winston glanced at the clock and gave a cry.

"It's surely the Duke. He said he might stop by."

The Duke was then announced. He came loudly in,
sporting velvet trousers and a purple waistcoat.

He kissed Mrs. Winston's hand and Madelina's.

"Glad to see you home, Miss Madelina."

"Thank you, Duke," Madelina managed a smile.

The Duke cast a look at Mrs. Winston and that lady
immediately rose. It was now or never, she knew.

"I'll just – er go and er – "

Her voice trailed off and she left the room giving no
excuse whatsoever.

Madelina, head lowered, heard a strange creaking
sound. She looked up to find the Duke on his knees.

His face said it all.

"Dearest! At last I have you to myself. And I must ask you – " Here the Duke shifted a little with a cracking of his knees. "I must ask you if you will be my wife."

She heard his proposal as a prisoner might hear the slam of a prison door.

Her right hand strayed towards the magazine she had cast aside, the magazine that announced the betrothal of Oliver de Burge and Lady Kitty.

Its touch seemed to decide her.

"Yes, Duke," she said simply and without emotion. "Thank – you. I will."

CHAPTER EIGHT

The triumphant outcome of her plotting sent Mrs. Winston into a fever of activity. Dressmakers, hat-makers and shoemakers were immediately summoned to the house.

She was determined that her stepdaughter should have the finest trousseau possible and had no qualms at all in spending Madelina's own money for the purpose.

Madelina baulked at a fancy Reception and in the end Mrs. Winston agreed that the Wedding guests would return to the house for the Wedding breakfast.

She decided that she would employ a French chef and spent hours poring over menus.

The Wedding date was set for March 5th and, when Mrs. Winston broached the subject of a honeymoon to the Duke, he looked somewhat abashed. He had to admit that he did not have 'the readies' at his disposal.

"Oh, don't you bother your head about that, Duke," she simpered. "You know there's a way round that!"

The way round was, of course, to further dip into Madelina's fortune. Until the girl was twenty-one Mrs. Winston had full control of her account.

Madelina well knew that she was paying for every aspect of her own Wedding. She did not care.

It loomed at the very far edge of her expectations.

Perhaps the dreaded day would never arrive.

She had said 'yes' because she had not been able to think of any reason to say 'no', because the only man she wished to marry could never be hers.

Mrs. Winston was set against returning to Albany and in her deepest being Madelina began to feel the same.

What was there for her in Albany? Those friends she had once had were no doubt being married themselves – and theirs would be love matches. And she did not think she could bear witnessing anyone else's happiness.

She might as well stay in England. She might as well marry the Duke and the intimacy that marriage would necessarily entail she tried to put out of her mind.

The Duke decided that Brighton would be a good place for a honeymoon and set about hiring a house on the seafront. Although the Wedding was not until March, he took the house at once.

He had heard that the gambling scene in Brighton was first rate and he might as well see if he could swell his own pitiful funds while waiting for Madelina's.

Now he had secured Madelina, he was beginning to feel somewhat restless. Dash it, a gentleman needed some distractions that a female did not need. So he decided to stay in Brighton until Christmas Eve.

Madelina was not at all sorry to see him go. He had taken to whistling and he would cheerfully regale anyone present with an entire range of music hall melodies.

Mrs. Winston naturally found it charming and beat along with her lorgnette, but Madelina began to think that she would scream and once or twice had to leave the room.

She would slip into the small walled garden at the rear of the house and stand there miserably in the cold.

Before the Duke departed, he and Mrs. Winston discussed the guest list for the Wedding.

The Duke seemed as anxious as Madelina that there should be 'no great fuss' and in the end the list comprised his two great-aunts, an uncle, seven old friends and Lady Bamber.

He mooted the idea of Earl Villers, but Madelina made a swift protest and to her relief, Mrs. Winston agreed.

If the Earl was invited, they would have to invite Lady Kitty. And in that case, they could not avoid asking her fiancé, Mr. Oliver de Burge.

*

Lady Bamber returned from Paris four days before Christmas. She immediately sent a letter to Mrs. Winston, in which she discreetly enquired after Madelina.

Madelina had not written to her since she had left Belmont, but Lady Bamber had heard from the Duke that Miss Winston was 'recuperating' after an illness.

Mrs. Winston had agreed with those appraised of the secret that it was in nobody's interest to trumpet abroad news of the blood relationship between Madelina and de Burge. Neither was it in anybody's interest to reveal that the two of them had forged a romance.

This decision of Mrs. Winston's was as much out of self-interest as concern for Madelina's reputation. She had no desire to be the widow of an out-and-out cad!

There had not been even a hint of a romance in the air the last time Lady Bamber saw Madelina and de Burge together – the day she left Belmont Hall for Paris.

So she would not suspect that Madelina's illness and the person of de Burge were in any way connected. And Mrs. Winston's reply to Lady Bamber was therefore circumspect.

She put it down to Madelina nursing a seemingly hopeless love for Duke Tunney. The Duke, she said, had come to his senses once Madelina had left Belmont and his proposal had restored Madelina's health, but it would not be wise to dwell on the subject in her presence.

Madelina was blissfully unaware of this fiction, but was glad to hear that Lady Bamber was in London again.

She visited the very next day and Mrs. Winston just happened to be out shopping, so then Lady Bamber found Madelina alone in the drawing room.

Her practised eye immediately told her that all was not well with her cousin. She remembered a girl with great vitality and this was missing in the pale composed young lady seated on the sofa.

Madelina rose to embrace her visitor.

"Oh, how I have missed you!" she lamented.

"And I have missed you, my dear," replied Lady Bamber. After a kiss she held Madelina at arm's length with a slight frown. "Happy?"

"Oh, yes I am!" Madelina's voice was unnaturally bright. "Shall I ring for tea?"

"Yes lovely, thank you." Lady Bamber sat down and Madelina rang the bell to summon Beth.

"How did you find your mother-in-law?" she asked.

Lady Bamber gave a smile.

"Ailing. But she rallied, and was still alive when I left her last week. I don't plan to return until the spring, so I shall be in London for your Wedding."

Madelina was silent as Lady Bamber cast around for something else to say when Beth arrived. She appeared relieved at the distraction and asked for tea and fruit loaf.

Lady Bamber crossed her hands over in her lap and waited until Beth had gone before trying another tack.

"I was frankly quite astonished to hear that you and the Duke are to marry," she said quietly.

Madelina looked up sharply.

"You – disapprove? You think I accepted because of – his title?"

Lady Bamber shook her head slowly.

"I know you well enough now to be certain that would not be your motive. I assume it's love."

Madelina then flushed horribly.

It was quite enough to convince Lady Bamber that Mrs. Winston's story of her 'seemingly hopeless love' for the Duke was a fabrication.

At the same time she was equally convinced that the stepmother's admonition that it would be best 'not to dwell on the subject' was correct.

Something was wrong and it was causing obvious distress to Madelina to discuss the Wedding. She therefore turned the conversation to other matters, Paris, Christmas and all the entertainment that London could offer.

Beth returned with the tea at the same time as Mrs. Winston arrived back. She looked somewhat alarmed to find Madelina alone with Lady Bamber and what might have been discussed between them.

Lady Bamber was quick to reassure Mrs. Winston,

"We have been talking about my trip to Paris and all kinds of things. I haven't had a chance to ask Madelina about the Wedding yet."

Mrs. Winston relaxed.

"Oh, I'll get Beth to take my packages upstairs and then we'll all have a nice chat together."

Madelina rose.

"I am going to retire to my room, Stepmama. I'll take up your packages."

Lady Bamber rose to kiss Madelina before she left and then remarked,

"Now that your stepmother is here, I shall bring up the subject of my New Year's Eve ball. It is to be held at my house in Berkeley Square and I have an invitation here in my purse. I do hope you will both come. The Duke, of course, has his own invitation."

"How very kind of you!" Mrs. Winston burbled. "We would be delighted."

Madelina opened her mouth as if to protest, but then seemed to think better of it.

"Thank you, Cousin," she said simply and, after a quick kiss, left the room with Beth in tow.

Lady Bamber's eyes followed after her.

"How do you find her?" asked Mrs. Winston

"Somewhat subdued for a young girl about to be married," Lady Bamber could not help but reply.

Mrs. Winston looked taken aback.

"She has much matured since you saw her last," she explained awkwardly after a moment.

Lady Bamber raised an eyebrow, but said nothing. They sat in silence for a moment until a sudden unwelcome thought seemed to strike Mrs. Winston.

"And who else have you invited to your ball?" she asked with an anxious tone that surprised Lady Bamber.

"There will be quite a number of guests. I would need my list in front of me to recall all the names."

"Of course. Of course." Mrs. Winston sniffed.

Lady Bamber detected that Mrs. Winston wanted to know whether someone *in particular* was to be at the ball, but did not know how to ask without revealing the person's identity.

Lady Bamber wondered if this person was in some way connected to the change in Madelina, but instinctively felt that she should not enquire further.

Mrs. Winston was, of course, thinking of de Burge. Lady Kitty and Earl Villers were bound to be invited. She was so worried that the shock of seeing de Burge would set Madelina back.

Then again, Madelina was bound to run into them sooner or later at parties and, as long as it was at public events, what harm could it really do?

Particularly as she was now safely engaged to be married, perhaps it would be as well to get the unpleasant encounter out of the way.

Once she was introduced to the delights of married life, Oliver de Burge would surely be forever relegated to the past. After all one man's embrace could utterly erase the memory of another.

Madelina had also considered the possibility that de Burge and Lady Kitty would be at the ball. She had been going to refuse the invitation, but had been unable to think of a suitable excuse. Nearer the time she would plead a cold. That would be the best thing to do.

And yet – and yet – the longing to see him one more time was still there even if it was at a distance! She had been trying so hard to banish him from her thoughts, but the idea of a glimpse of his face set her heart racing.

He would be at the ball as the fiancé of Lady Kitty, of course. That would be a distressing enough spectacle.

But would he be equally distressed to see her there as the fiancée of the Duke?

'Perhaps he will not come to the ball,' she decided at last. 'Perhaps the knowledge that I will be present will discourage him. He will know that I am bound to be there as Lady Bamber's relation and he will feign illness rather than embarrass me.'

It was with this thought in her mind that she went to her window as she heard Lady Bamber departing.

Madelina watched the carriage drive away.

Snow fluttered silently down, the flakes illuminated in the gas flare from the street lamps.

The street was empty and silent.

Empty and silent as Madelina felt her own heart to be in her aching breast.

*

Christmas passed quietly at Wigmore Street.

Mrs. Winston had not been long enough in London to have made many friends and those few invitations she did receive she politely declined on Madelina's account.

The fact was that Mrs. Winston wanted to wait until she could sally forth into Society as the stepmother to a Duchess. Until then she was content to remain somewhat secluded for the moment.

Lady Bamber's ball would suffice as Madelina's first public appearance as the Duke's fiancée.

The Duke duly returned to London from Brighton as he had promised on Christmas Eve.

He stayed at his Pall Mall flat, but came every day to Wigmore Street.

Madelina stirred herself to decorate a tree with Beth and hang garlands about the house. Mrs. Winston ordered in a succulent turkey and cases of wine from Fortnum's.

The Duke, who would usually spend Christmas at Belmont, said that he was delighted with the company and the Seasonal fare.

He had experienced a run of good luck at Brighton, and so had bought a number of presents without recourse to Mrs. Winston's purse.

Madelina received a splendid ruby brooch and Mrs. Winston a necklace of jet. Even Beth was not forgotten and received a pretty little cameo.

"I still ain't sure about him, though," she confessed later to her young Mistress.

"What do you mean, Beth?" asked Madelina.

"I means that he ain't good enough for you, miss," answered Beth fiercely.

Madelina stared at her pale face in the mirror. She seemed to have lost her lustre and she was certain that she looked ten years older.

It was a miracle that the Duke still cared for her at all, she thought, although she did not say so to Beth.

*

It started to snow in earnest again after Christmas and Mrs. Winston felt that the weather over the next few days would not be very good for shopping and thought that Madelina should choose a dress from her trousseau.

"There's a rather fine, violet-coloured, silk evening gown," she reminded Madelina. "And a gold muslin. The dressmaker will have to get a move on, but I'm sure that she could have one of them ready in time."

Since she had by now convinced herself that Oliver de Burge would not as a matter of principle attend the ball, Madelina had no interest in how she might look on the day. But she chose the violet silk to please her stepmother.

The Duke did not keep his own carriage in town, and so hired a suitable conveyance for the event.

He arrived early, as some roads were impassable and the coach driver would have to take a circuitous route to Berkeley Square.

Madelina sat across from him, wrapped in a warm velvet-lined cloak.

Beth had been determined that her Mistress should look her very best despite Madelina's indifference. She had washed and brushed her hair and put it in a coil on the nape of her neck, pinning on a silver tiara at the end.

The violet silk softened even further the hue of her skin. And Beth had insisted on dabbing a little rouge onto her lips and the merest hint of kohl on her eyelids.

The Duke had given a whistle when his fiancée descended the stairs.

"I shall be the proudest fellow at the ball," he said, kissing her gloved hand.

In the carriage he gazed at her all the way until she felt acutely uncomfortable. He seemed to be sizing up his prize she could not help but think to herself.

She supposed that Lady Kitty and her father would be at the ball and steeled herself. She would be as polite as possible and would remove herself from them quickly.

She had not been to Lady Bamber's house till now and marvelled at its grandeur as the carriage drew up.

There was a long line of carriages ahead of them and they had to wait their turn to stop at the front door where footmen would open the carriage door for them.

Madelina could watch the guests ahead step out of their conveyances. She felt over-awed at the elegance and sophistication of the ladies.

At the same time the rouge on her lips suddenly felt wrong and she took out a handkerchief and surreptitiously wiped it away. She dared not attempt to do the same for her eyes for fear that, without a mirror, she might simply smear the kohl over her cheeks.

At last their carriage reached the head of the line. A footman bowed and then handed Mrs. Winston down, followed by Madelina and next the Duke.

The front door stood open. Chandeliers in the great hall beyond gleamed, their light flowing out into the cold night and down the front steps like a river of gold.

Madelina made her way slowly up on the Duke's arm. Within she heard violins tuning up and her mind at once leapt to the evening at Belmont when she had danced in de Burge's arms.

The grand reception room in which the ball was to take place was on the first floor. Madelina and the Duke, followed by Mrs. Winston swept towards it up the stairs.

"The Duke of Belmont and his companions, Mrs. Harriet Winston and Miss Madelina Winston," the butler announced in loud stentorian tones.

Madelina stood blinking on the threshold. People turned and a murmur of appreciation ran through the room.

She hardly heard it.

Her eyes had settled on a figure just by the door, a figure whose outline seemed to scorch itself so painfully on her senses that she thought she would cry out.

It was Oliver de Burge.

He had come to the ball, despite her conviction to the contrary.

And on his arm hung Lady Kitty Villers, dressed in a dark-red satin, her eyes glittering like a cobra's as she surveyed her erstwhile rival.

Madelina could not help but notice that de Burge looked shocked to see her.

He seemed to throw an almost accusing glance at Lady Kitty, before shaking himself free of her grip and moving away into the crowd.

Lady Kitty gave a slight smile, bowed her head at Madelina and took off after him.

She had no time to wonder at this little scene, for Lady Bamber had sailed up to her with coos of approval.

"My dear, you look divine, simply divine! I am so delighted to welcome you here to my home, which you must think of as your home too whenever you need it."

Duke Tunney and Mrs. Winston exchanged glances interpreting this as a strong indication that Lady Bamber would make Madelina her heir.

Madelina thanked her cousin profusely and added,

"Our house in Wigmore Street is very comfortable. But it is nothing like so – grand. This is truly gracious."

Lady Bamber beamed.

"It is surely graced with your presence this evening. Now come. I must introduce you and your stepmother and the Duke, your fiancé, to my friends."

The next hour or so seemed just a blur to Madelina. Face after face loomed towards her, she made curtsey after curtsey to Lord this, Lady that, Viscount this, Countess that until her head fairly reeled.

Duke Tunney was known by a great many of the guests and Madelina noticed that some of them looked a little askance when he presented her as his fiancée.

It was clear that they thought that the Duke had the best of the bargain.

Mrs. Winston also noticed and began to wonder if she might have been a little hasty in her pursuit of the first Duke she had met. After all here were hundreds of titled gentlemen, many unattached and most of them obviously taken with her beautiful young stepdaughter.

Still the Duke had been easy prey and he obviously appreciated his catch. Which was more than could be said for her stepdaughter.

Madelina seemed to be worryingly preoccupied, as her eyes flew hither and thither, hardly resting a second on the person she was being introduced to.

Mrs. Winston, overwhelmed at the sight of so much aristocratic blood, when arriving at the ballroom, had not seen de Burge and Lady Kitty, but she assumed that they were around here somewhere. And also assumed that it was they whom Madelina was seeking.

There was music before supper but no dancing and, when supper was announced, the Duke escorted Madelina to the dining hall, whilst Mrs. Winston was assigned to the care of an elderly Ambassador friend of Lady Bamber's.

Lady Bamber, totally unaware of the situation that existed between her cousin and her friends, de Burge and Lady Kitty, had innocently placed these three near to each other at the table as she felt that Madelina would appreciate being seated with people she had met before.

Even the Duke froze as he realised the unwitting *faux pas*. It was too late to make a scene, so he drew out Madelina's chair.

Cold with horror, she sat down.

De Burge was seated to her right, so close that she could feel his shoulder brushing against hers. Lady Kitty sat opposite de Burge and Earl Villers sat to the right of his daughter and opposite Madelina.

The Duke had a seat on Madelina's left with Mrs. Winston to his left.

De Burge gave a curt nod of greeting to the latest arrivals, whilst Lady Kitty merely regarded them with cool amusement across the table.

Madelina plucked up the courage to speak first.

"I thought that you would not be here tonight," she said to de Burge in an undertone.

"And I thought that *you* would not be here tonight," he returned. "I was informed so, anyway."

"By whom?" Madelina frowned

There was a pause, and then de Burge replied in an almost bitter tone.

"By Lady Kitty."

Although startled that de Burge had alluded to his fiancée as *Lady* Kitty rather than just Kitty, Madelina could not disguise an equally bitter tone in her own voice as she responded,

"What made you imagine that she would know?"

"She said she had been told so by Lady Bamber," began de Burge and then he broke off.

Madelina stole a glance at him, which he met. His black eyes looked like stone, unreflecting and hard.

"Oh, what the deuce does it matter!" he finished, and angrily shook out his napkin.

Turning away, Madelina saw that Lady Kitty was watching and the smile playing on her lips told her all.

Madelina's assumption that he would not come to the ball if he had known that she would be here had been correct.

Lady Kitty had lied to him to make sure that he attended. She had wanted him to be here so that she could flaunt her hold over him to Madelina.

And de Burge had just guessed as much himself.

"What a merry party we're going to be," Lady Kitty now trilled, leaning back as crab soup was served to her.

"Aren't we just!" Madelina heard de Burge mutter.

She lowered her head miserably. His behaviour towards her was far from friendly and seeing him here with Lady Kitty, she was beginning to feel unfriendly in return.

Must they hate each other because they could not love in the manner they wished?

The Duke strained to listen. The fact that they had barely spoken disturbed him more than if they had engaged in relaxed conversation.

'The devil can take her if she still has a yen for de Burge,' he thought disagreeably!

He turned to speak sharply to Madelina when her bowl of soup arrived and she did not respond.

"Madam, what distracts you so much that you don't acknowledge this fellow?"

Madelina looked round wildly.

"W-what fellow?"

Seeing the server waiting patiently at her side, she apologised and pulled her bowl towards her.

De Burge had turned at the Duke's harsh tone, but he could not see him as Madelina sat between them. A furrow appeared on his brow and, although he reached for his spoon, he did not touch the soup.

Lady Kitty, watching, seemed to make a decision. Leaning across the table, her face swimming into the light shed by the silver candelabra, she addressed Madelina in a tone as sweet as syrup,

"Is it a strange experience to be sitting next to a brother you never knew you had?"

A shudder went through Madelina.

Without thinking she thrust her chair back, rose up and hurried away down the length of the hall.

A startled footmen threw open the door to let her through.

Lady Bamber, from the head of the table, watched with a frown on her fine features.

CHAPTER NINE

Mrs. Winston was naturally mortified that Madelina had caused such a stir at the table, but she did not wish to compound the drama by chasing after her.

The Duke was equally determined to act as if her flight was perfectly innocent, explaining to all and sundry that she had suddenly felt a little faint and had gone to take some air.

De Burge listened with a grim expression and his eyes strayed to the door as if he was inclined to follow suit.

Lady Bamber, however, did not believe the Duke's explanation.

Having made sure that her guests were served with the next course, she quietly placed her napkin on the table and slipped from the dining hall.

She found Madelina curled up on a *chaise longue* in a room set aside for the ladies, face hidden in the crook of her arm.

"What's the matter, Madelina?" she asked, taking a seat on the end of the *chaise longue*.

Madelina raised a tear-stained face.

"Nothing I can speak of."

"Not even to me?"

"Especially – not to you," said Madelina miserably.

Lady Bamber considered for a moment.

She had deduced from Mrs. Winston's query as to who else might be at the ball that Madelina had formed an attachment to someone she knew.

An attachment that for some reason was not to be countenanced. Who could this secret man be? She knew that Madelina had spent most of her time since arriving in England at Belmont Hall.

That narrowed the possibilities down considerably. As she thought about it, there was only one possibility –

"Oliver de Burge!" she cried triumphantly.

Madelina's shocked expression at the sound of this name was confirmation enough.

Lady Bamber then reached her hand forward and gently laid it on Madelina's arm.

"If you feel so strongly for him, my dear, as your face suggests you do, why did you then agree to marry the Duke? Because Oliver became engaged to Lady Kitty?"

Madelina gave a nod. That would suffice surely.

But not for Lady Bamber, who gave a faint snort as she considered it.

"Knowing Oliver as I do," she said, "it's as unlikely that he is in love with Lady Kitty as it is that you are in love with the Duke. And I find it strange that you are both engaged to people you don't care for."

Madelina now found that she could not refute Lady Bamber's comment that she did not care for the Duke, as it was all too true.

Instead she fixed her eyes on her cousin.

"Y-you know Oliver well?"

"He was at boarding school in Gloucestershire and spent his summers at Belmont with his cousins, the Duke's family. He and the Duke would often come over to me at nearby Cressy Manor."

Madelina was puzzled.

"Why did he not go home to his own parents?"

"They lived too far to North in Carlisle. Besides, as is commonly known, he never got on well with his mother and there was little love lost between him and his father."

Madelina wondered what Lady Bamber would say if she knew that Mr. de Burge was not Oliver's father.

This led her to wonder whether her cousin knew anything at all about the relationship that had once existed between his real father – her own, Mr. Winston and his mother, Mrs. de Burge.

"Did you – did you ever meet Oliver's mother?"

Lady Bamber looked at her quickly and answered,

"Never. And she never entered Society."

"Why?"

"She had something – of a history," Lady Bamber replied.

"May I hear it?" Fearing that she might sound too eager, Madelina tempered her tone. "I-I am interested in anything that concerns Oliver."

"Well," she began, "the fact is, Mrs. de Burge was once known as Adelaide Anderson, a dancer at the *Café Angel* in Soho."

"I-I see," Madelina stammered.

Lady Bamber rose and went across to the dressing table where she rearranged the bowls and pin boxes.

From this Madelina read that Lady Bamber did not know how best to deliver the next part of her story. It had to be because it was about Mr. Winston himself and his involvement with – Adelaide Anderson.

"A young man of good family became infatuated with Miss Anderson," Lady Bamber said at last. "He even proposed marriage. His parents very strongly disapproved as one might imagine."

She paused to catch her breath and then went on,

"The young man refused to be cowed by them and a Wedding date was set. Then, for whatever reason, he abruptly broke off all relations with Miss Anderson and left the country. She quickly found solace in the arms of Cecil de Burge, a wealthy but reclusive gentleman. He swept her off to Carlisle, where he kept her pretty much hidden, no doubt because of her background. It was in Carlisle that she gave birth to Oliver."

Madelina listened with bated breath. If this 'young man' was her own father, then it was obvious that Lady Bamber did not know that the reason he had broken off all relations with Miss Adelaide Anderson was because he had discovered that she was expecting his child.

"The young man who was so infatuated with Miss Anderson," she enquired softly, "you said left the country."

Lady Bamber looked uneasy.

"Yes."

"Where did he go?"

"America."

Madelina dropped her gaze. It was all exactly as she had been told at Belmont Hall.

She must have been nurturing an unconscious hope that the tale of her father's relationship with Mrs. de Burge might be false for her to feel as desolate as this to hear it confirmed by her own cousin.

Watching her, Lady Bamber guessed that nothing she had told Madelina had come as a surprise. The girl already knew all and, moreover, knew that the gentleman in question was her own father.

"How did you find out, Madelina?"

Madelina looked up guiltily and then gave a sigh of admission. There was no point denying what her face had obviously already revealed to her perceptive cousin.

"Mrs. de Burge told my stepmother, who told me."

She did not, of course, add that part of the story which she had sworn to keep secret, the part that concerned Oliver's true parentage.

Lady Bamber shook her head, puzzled.

"When did Mrs. de Burge tell your stepmother?"

Madelina shifted uneasily on the *chaise longue.*

"She – came to Belmont while I was there."

"She did? That's astonishing. She never goes into Society, as I told you. And to come all that way South!"

"Lady Kitty invited her," confessed Madelina after a moment.

An expression crossed Lady Bamber's features that indicated that the situation was suddenly very clear to her.

"So Lady Kitty found a way of putting a spoke in the wheel! I have underestimated her. Though I cannot see why the fact that Oliver's mother once had a dalliance with your father should be sufficient grounds to keep you apart. Not after all these years. Is it Mrs. de Burge who came to that conclusion or your stepmother?"

"Both," said Madelina truthfully.

"Does Oliver know the story too?"

"Yes."

Fearful that further probing by Lady Bamber would lead to the uncovering of the full story, Madelina changed tack.

"Did you know at the time it happened about my father and – Miss Anderson?"

Lady Bamber gave a sad nod.

"I was only recently married. My husband, Lord Bamber, did not wish his name to become embroiled in the scandal and took me off to the Continent. When I returned, the affair was over and your father had left for America. I think your father was bitter that the little family he had in England had seen fit to disown him over the matter. At any rate he did not communicate with them for some time and, when at last he wrote, it was too late – they were dead. He had long lost contact with me."

Touched by this confession and anxious to hide the tears that sprang to her eyes, Madelina rose from the *chaise longue*.

Lady Bamber then made up her mind.

"Well, dear, since you know this much, I might as well get you a ticket for Oswald Vane's new play, which opens tomorrow," she said.

"Oswald Vane? A play?" Madelina stared.

"Apparently his play is based on the story between your father and Mrs. de Burge – although the names are all changed, of course."

Madelina gasped.

"The story is such – common knowledge?"

"Oh, at the time, yes, but not now," Lady Bamber hastily reassured her. "No one will make the connection. But Oswald Vane knew your father well as they were at school together. So you may find the evening of interest."

Madelina felt sick at the thought that her father's sad tale was to be played out in front of total strangers.

And suppose that this Oswald Vane knew the *whole* story and knew that when Adelaide married de Burge she was already carrying young Mr. Winston's child? Would he be so cruel as to relate the full events onstage?

Lady Bamber eyed her with concern.

"My dear, I would not have told you about it at all, but since you know the story already and seem to be keen to learn more – "

Her voice trailed away as there came a knock at the door and a maid-servant put her head round.

"Beg pardon, my Lady, but I've been lookin' all over for you. We're on to dessert and your guests are now wonderin' – "

"Oh my, goodness me. I was completely taken up. Madelina, dear, I must go down."

"Do, Cousin. I will follow you shortly." Madelina nodded.

Lady Bamber, mortified that she had forsaken her role as hostess for so long, flew from the room.

Madelina went to the mirror. In the glass she saw a wretchedly pale face and tidied herself as best she could.

Then she opened the door and stepped out.

From far below came the sound of people enjoying their supper and she rushed down the stairs, intending to call at once for the carriage. She would go home and send the carriage back for her stepmother and the Duke.

As she reached the hall, a man sitting in a huge old-fashioned sedan, rose from its depths.

It was Oliver de Burge.

"I waited to see you," he said simply.

"You should – not have," Madelina whispered.

"I should not have," he agreed, but his eyes spoke otherwise.

Without taking her eyes from de Burge, Madelina signalled to a footman, who opened the door and went out onto the top step, where he whistled for her carriage.

"You are leaving so soon?" de Burge asked.

"Yes, I am."

He gave a short nod.

"Kitty should not have spoken as she did," he said.

"No," Madelina could not help but agree.

They stood in silence, so still that each could hear the other's breath. Then both made to speak at once,

"Are you happy – ?"

They broke off, equally abashed.

"I am perfectly happy," Madelina said after a while.

"You are?"

"The Duke is very attentive."

De Burge could not help himself.

"He is too coarse for you."

"And Lady Kitty is too possessive of you," shot back Madelina.

He looked angry.

"I am as happy with her as you are with the Duke," he replied after a moment.

Madelina felt a sob of desolation rise in her throat at his words.

It was almost with relief that she heard the sound of wheels drawing up at the door.

"Goodbye," she muttered.

"Goodbye."

Madelina did not look back, but fled to the safety of the carriage.

At home a surprised Beth answered the door with a lamp in her hand.

"What? Back so soon, miss? And alone?"

"Yes. Help me undress, Beth, and then you may go to bed. And send the carriage back to Berkeley Square."

*

Early the next morning, Mrs. Winston pounced on Madelina where she breakfasted in her room.

"Why on earth did you leave without telling us?"

Madelina tapped the shell of her egg with the back of her spoon.

"I could not bear to be in the presence of Mr. de Burge and Lady Kitty."

"It seemed that they could not bear to be in our company either for they too left early," Mrs. Winston said.

"Was the ball a success?" Madelina asked politely, although she was thinking about de Burge and Lady Kitty. "Was Lady Bamber pleased?"

"I should hope so!" sniffed Mrs Winston. "It was still going on when the Duke and I left at midnight. By the way – " She searched in her reticule and drew something out. "This is for you."

Madelina opened the envelope. Her heart gave a sudden thud as she read the enclosed card. She was invited to Lady Bamber's box on that very evening for the opening performance of a play by Oswald Vane.

The play was called *The Secret Wound.*

*

Mrs. Winston was piqued to learn that she was not invited to the theatre as well.

Madelina was surprised at the omission. Perhaps it was because of the nature of the play.

However the Duke came to the rescue by promising to take Mrs. Winston to the Music Hall.

Lady Bamber had written that she would send her own carriage for Madelina, as she was being escorted to the theatre by Oswald Vane himself.

It was a cold evening and snow was falling again.

So Madelina dressed in a gown of dark green crepe with a pretty bonnet, muff and cloak of white ermine. Her stepmother insisted she wear the brooch that the Duke had given her.

The Duke had dined with them before taking Mrs. Winston to the Music Hall in London's East End.

He gazed approvingly at Madelina as she entered the drawing room.

"Gad, you're a regular little beauty in that white fur. Like a white doe," he exclaimed. "If I saw you at a distance, mind, I might shoot you!"

The Duke chuckled at his own joke, glancing all the while at Mrs. Winston, who was at the window watching out for Lady Bamber's carriage.

"See how Madelina is wearing your brooch, Duke," Mrs. Winston then pointed out.

The Duke at once put out his hand and drew aside Madelina's cloak, too quickly for her to protest. The ruby brooch was pinned on the collar of her gown, just below her throat.

The Duke's eyes lingered there and then he let the cloak close again over her.

"It's so hard for a man to wait," he murmured to Madelina with a leer.

She shuddered and then drew the cloak even tighter around her.

"It's very good of Lady Bamber to have invited you tonight," commented Mrs. Winston. "Did she say what the play was about, my dear?"

Madelina coloured slightly and moved quickly to the fire to warm her hands.

"I hardly know, Stepmama," she replied over her shoulder. "A love affair – I think."

"That's all this fellow ever writes about," remarked the Duke, his eyes still fixed on Madelina.

"I should like to have seen it all the same," sighed Mrs. Winston. "I'm partial to stories of love."

"No changing your mind at this late hour then, Mrs. Winston!" chided the Duke.

"All the same," said Mrs. Winston again.

Madelina bit her lip anxiously and prayed,

'Please don't let Stepmama and the Duke turn up at the theatre. There might be a scene if she worked out that the subject of the play was her late husband's affair with Mrs. de Burge, when she was called Adelaide Anderson!'

The arrival of Lady Bamber's carriage distracted Mrs. Winston for the moment.

"Here it is," she cried. "With a crest on the door!"

She pressed closer to the window pane to watch it draw up at the house and then gave a puzzled exclamation.

"But it's empty!"

"Yes, indeed," Madelina said, "Lady Bamber will meet me there. She is being escorted by Mr. Oswald Vane himself."

Mrs. Winston turned from the window, a furrow on her brow.

"Oswald Vane? The name seems familiar to me – "

Madelina, to avoid a reply, hurried to the drawing room door and tugged it open.

"Enjoy the Music Hall," she called and fled.

As the carriage drove away, she saw her stepmother watching from the window.

She had not been to the theatre in London yet and marvelled at the elegant crowd teeming on the pavement.

The coachman helped her out and into the foyer, where she showed the invitation card to a doorman.

"Ah, Lady Bamber's box," he said and beckoned to a young usher who led her up some red carpeted stairs.

"Has Lady Bamber arrived yet?" asked Madelina.

"She'll not be in her box tonight," the usher replied. "She's with Mr. Vane. But the other gentleman's arrived."

"The – other gentleman?"

"Yes, miss. Here we are."

The usher threw open a door and Madelina stepped through as a figure already seated there rose in greeting.

It was Oliver de Burge.

He looked as shocked to see Madelina as she felt to see him. She backed towards the door as if to escape, only to hear it close behind the departing usher.

Madelina's mind was in turmoil. Lady Bamber had planned this and in ignorance of the full facts.

She had wanted to give the two of them a chance to meet in private, not realising that the bond between them was such that to be thrown together like this was nothing short of cruelty.

Madelina felt for the doorknob just behind her. Her fingers closed around it, but she hesitated to turn it.

The agony in de Burge's eyes transfixed her. All his resolution was as nothing now she was with him again.

"Stay," he commanded huskily.

"If – we are seen," she whispered, her eyes straying towards the audience gathering beyond the box.

"What harm is it if we are?" de Burge gave a short bitter laugh. "We are related, after all."

"They don't know that."

"No," he conceded reluctantly.

"And you said we should not meet until – "

"Until our love for each other was ripped from our hearts?" he finished for her fiercely. "Well it is. Isn't it?"

"Y-yes," she lied.

"After all, you are happy. And I am happy. And we are both safely engaged to be married to the Duke and Lady Kitty respectively. Are we not?"

Madelina lowered her eyes.

"Yes."

"So what harm will it do to enjoy a play together?"

The thought struck Madelina that it would be an act of cowardice to flee and leave Oliver to watch the play alone and to follow alone the dreadful narrative of their own father's deceit. Perhaps he was not even aware that this was to be the subject of the play!

Her hand fell from the doorknob and she took a step forward.

"Oliver," she enquired in a low voice, "did Lady Bamber tell you what this play is about?"

De Burge looked surprised.

"No. She invited me last night as Kitty and I were just leaving the ball. Kitty mentioned that she had a dinner engagement tonight with friends and, hearing that I was to be alone, Lady Bamber asked me join her here."

His brow furrowed as he reconsidered the fact that Madelina was also alone.

"She did not invite the Duke, either?"

"No. Nor my stepmother."

"Strange!" he exclaimed.

Madelina cast around for a way of explaining the situation that would not reveal how she had more or less confessed her feelings for him to Lady Bamber.

She decided to let the matter rest for the moment. It was more important to prepare Oliver – her brother – for the ordeal ahead.

Moving to her chair, she sat down, first taking up a programme lying on the seat. Her gaze was still on Oliver as she flicked thoughtlessly through its pages.

"Do you know the author of the play?" she asked.

"Oswald? I have met him once or twice at Lady Bamber's."

"Did he ever speak to you about – our father?"

He flinched at that '*our father*', as did Madelina in saying it. No more final a door could slam on their once romantic attachment than the sound of those two words.

"No, Madelina. Why should he?"

"Because he knew him since childhood and he has based this play tonight on my – our – father's liaison with your mother."

The blood drained from de Burge's features.

"The devil he has! Does he know that I am – "

"The result of that liaison? No. Lady Bamber does not know either."

De Burge gave a sardonic laugh.

"Yet she obviously thought that we might benefit in some way from having the facts thrust into our faces!"

Madelina was saved from having to confess that Lady Bamber had another motive entirely, that she had in fact thought that she was arranging a lovers' tryst, by the sound of the final bell announcing curtain up.

The audience began to settle and the lights faded.

Darkness had almost completely descended on the auditorium when there came the sound of a commotion at the entrance. A couple were arriving late.

Madelina peered over the balcony and froze.

There below, squeezing past the irate audience, was a large familiar figure with a plump whiskered gentleman in tow.

It was Mrs. Winston and the Duke! She must have changed her mind at the last minute and come here.

Whether in search of Madelina or not, the Duke's eye flitted over the audience and then up to the boxes.

Madelina quickly drew back. She prayed that she had not been seen, sitting there alone with Oliver de Burge.

De Burge had caught sight of the late arrivals and watched them with an amused expression.

"They were invited after all," he commented.

Madelina said nothing. The lights were dimmed, the curtain was rising and the stage was gradually revealed.

It could have been a drawing room in any smart London house with any one of a thousand grand old ladies standing at a window, but when young 'Mr. Wilton' was announced, Madelina's heart thudded painfully. Wilton!

There had been hardly any attempt to disguise her father's name. Here he was, depicted before her and, when the lady turned and called him 'son', Madelina knew that she was looking at a portrayal of the paternal grandmother she had never met.

The scene had barely begun when Madelina heard the door of the box behind her thrown open.

The light from the corridor that streamed through distracted some of the audience below, who looked up and cried 'hush' even before the Duke thundered out his anger.

"Well, madam, I might well have expected it! And you too, Cousin! Planning a little tryst behind our backs. Disgusting, when you know what you are to each other!"

The Duke seized Madelina's arm and dragged her up from the chair. De Burge rose in protest, but the box was small and there was little he could do, as the Duke pulled Madelina out into the corridor.

"You stay and watch the play!" he then hissed at de Burge. "Attempt to interfere and I'll reveal your dirty little secret to the world."

With that he slammed the door on de Burge and the sorry tale that was unfolding on the stage beyond.

CHAPTER TEN

Madelina struggled, but the Duke had such a tight hold on her that it was useless.

He hurried her along the corridor and out into the street, where Mrs. Winston waited at the open door of their carriage.

"So you did come after all!" commented Madelina bitterly.

"Yes, as soon as I recalled that your father once mentioned Oswald Vane as being an old friend of his," replied Mrs. Winston tartly. "Lady Bamber would know that the two were acquainted, in which case it seemed so strange that you should be invited to the play and not me!"

She paused and then rambled on,

"When we saw you and that man, de Burge, in the box together, I understood the reason! Your cousin, Lady Bamber, cannot have any idea of the facts to be arranging such a meeting behind my back."

"She doesn't," said Madelina stoutly, before being propelled roughly into the carriage seat. Mrs. Winston then followed. The Duke climbed in and the horses set off.

"Where are you taking me?" cried Madelina.

"For a little sea air," replied the Duke grimly.

"Beth will come on after with our wardrobe," added Mrs. Winston. "She will bring a gown for your Wedding. The Duke is of the opinion that we should bring the date forward to next week."

Next week! Madelina fell back against the seat.

"M-my trousseau will not be ready," she protested feebly.

The Duke looked unconcerned.

"I'm a full-blooded, hunting, shooting and fishing Englishman, Miss Winston. And I've waited patiently to take possession of you. Too patiently, some would say. If you don't want to be my wife, there's others who would, arriving here on every tide, as my one-time cousin, Mr. de Burge, kindly pointed out."

Mrs. Winston gave a nervous swallow. Matters had gone so far now that it would affect Madelina's reputation if the Duke was to throw her over.

"The Duke has the right to remove you from any scene of temptation, my dear," she now said to Madelina. "I mean, what would people say to see you out in public, unchaperoned, with a man other than your fiancé?"

"It was only the once," protested Madelina, but the Duke interposed,

"This is the best method of ensuring that *once* does not become *twice*!"

Madelina realised that there was no more to be said. Leaning back, she closed her eyes and gave herself up to the rocking motion of the carriage.

The two recent encounters with Oliver de Burge had awakened feelings that she dared not define. Every romantic impulse towards him she had quashed with great resolution and quite a few prayers, but his actual person could not but reflect badly upon the Duke.

De Burge was refined, principled and elegant. His bearing was more truly aristocratic than Duke Tunney's could ever be.

In fact if one stripped away the Duke's velvet coats, his expensive boots and silver-headed cane, he could, with his red cheeks, thick hands and damp moustache, easily be taken for a tapster at some country tavern!

This unkind, if accurate, assessment of the Duke's appearance almost served as a relief to Madelina's elastic nerves.

That is until she remembered that those thick hands would soon have the right to fondle her, those red cheeks would soon press themselves to hers, that damp moustache travel across her lips.

The thought made her mind reel.

She could not help but recall de Burge's restrained passion and the current that raced between his lips and hers when he had kissed her.

Perhaps she would discover a kind of oblivion in the Duke's arms.

She tried to imagine that her Wedding night with him would be so all-consuming, whether for good or ill, that it would drive all memory of de Burge out of her soul.

It was impossible for her not to wonder if Oliver too would seek the same closure of romantic memory with Lady Kitty.

Madelina had tried hard not to think of those two in each other's arms. She knew they had embraced, although she felt that Lady Kitty would always remain at a haughty distance.

But Lady Kitty could not then deny intimacy to her husband on their Wedding night!

Try as Madelina might to shrink from this line of thought, images assailed her with deadly power.

She could see a lavish room, perhaps a room at *The Langham.* She saw champagne in a silver bucket, she saw Oliver seated on a chair, waiting for his bride. The door opened and Lady Kitty wafted in, dressed in a white linen nightgown. Oliver rose to take her in his arms and carry her – carry her –

It was too much. Madelina's eyes flew open. She felt that she was no longer Mistress of her own mind!

It was dawn when the carriage rolled up before a handsome Regency house on the outskirts of Brighton.

The sea lay beyond a low railing on the other side of the street and Madelina was conducted to a bedroom by a sullen-looking footman.

*

She was so tired that she slept for the whole day, a curiously untroubled slumber.

It was dark when she awoke and she was delighted to see Beth appear in the room.

"One minute you was off to the theatre, the next I gets a message sayin' you was on your way to the seaside," Beth whispered, as if she imagined that the walls had ears.

"Lady Bamber called at the house and when I tells her you was gone off to Brighton she looks at me and she says, 'willingly, Beth?' and I looks right back and I says, 'I wouldn't think so, my Lady.' And without blinkin' an eye she says, 'tell Madelina she can always come to me'."

Beth fell silent for a moment, all the while gazing sadly at Madelina.

"Mrs. Winston wrote to bring your Weddin' gown with me. Is it certain, then? You're goin' to marry *him*."

Beth could not disguise her dislike of the Duke.

"Yes, Beth. It's certain and I think we had better agree to discuss him in a respectful manner in future, since he will soon be your Master as well as mine."

"Yes, miss," Beth mumbled without enthusiasm.

Madelina had resolved to accept her situation and honour her promise to marry the Duke. He had some good

146

qualities and she was sure that she would eventually learn to appreciate him.

Her resolution was put to a terrible test the very next day.

The Duke had business in town and only returned for dinner.

Mrs. Winston retired early and the Duke suggested a turn on the seafront, claiming that he wanted to show his fiancée the view.

Madelina agreed reluctantly and they set out at nine o'clock.

The moon was shining brightly and the sea beyond the seafront railing shimmered beneath its gleam.

Madelina felt a great calm settle over her as she and the Duke strolled along.

Coming to a gate in the railing, the Duke suggested that they take the path down to the beach.

Madelina hesitated to be in such a secluded place alone with the Duke, but she was eager to walk right at the water's edge and, believing that he would conduct himself as a gentleman, she rather reluctantly assented.

The path was steep and unlit, except by the moon, and the Duke insisted on taking her hand to guide her.

At one point her foot slipped and, as if he had been waiting for this moment, the Duke caught her at once by the waist to steady her.

"T-thank you," she said, trying to detach herself.

To her consternation, he would not let go. His grip on her waist tightened and he drew her close against him.

"Please let me go," said Madelina coldly. "This is no time for such – behaviour."

"It's the perfect time!" the Duke breathed. "Dark and private with no one about. Where else might I taste

147

in advance a little of what I shall have to the full in a few days' time?"

"W-what do you mean?" Madelina's heart shrank.

"I mean this!" crowed the Duke.

And then, forcing her head up with his free hand, he kissed her harshly on the lips. And his other hand now strayed from her waist and with horror she felt it creep towards her breasts.

Tearing her lips from his, she cried out angrily,

"Let me go, you – beast!"

"Beast, am I?" snarled the Duke. "Not such a beast that I try to claim the kind of caresses I'm sure you gave de Burge!"

Madelina put her two hands against his chest and with a supreme effort pushed him away.

"He – never demanded – anything!" she cried.

"I'm sure not," sneered the Duke. "I'm sure you played the wanton well enough with him."

Shocked beyond belief, Madelina turned and began to run back up the path.

With a loud curse he made to pursue her, but nature itself seemed to be on her side. Hearing another curse she turned briefly to see the Duke tugging at his cloak where it had caught on a furze bush.

She ran on. He must have freed himself, for she heard pebbles crunch from under his feet as he resumed his pursuit of her.

Reaching the gate, she flung herself through, then turned and held it tight, as if it would prove an unassailable barrier between herself and the Duke.

He was very near to her, puffing and wild-eyed. The moon slid behind a cloud and at that exact moment, the Duke lost his footing.

With a yell of rage and pain, as his ankle twisted in an ugly manner beneath him, he started to slide back down the path.

Madelina bent her head. There was no question but that she must go to his aid.

She was just about to open the gate when she heard voices on the path below. Someone was on their way up from the beach and had encountered the prostrate Duke and they were offering their help.

Madelina's heart gave a leap.

She was safe!

*

She hurried on back to the house where her wild ringing of the bell awakened Mrs. Winston and she was halfway down the stairs as the footman admitted her.

"What's the matter, Madelina? Where's the Duke?"

Madelina, panting heavily, then motioned her into the parlour where the footman could not overhear them.

"The Duke – tried to – assault me," Madelina burst out when the parlour door was closed behind them.

Mrs. Winston rocked on her feet for an instant and then took command of herself.

"Nonsense!" she refuted her fiercely. "You mistook his natural ardour for something else, that's all."

"Impossible," began Madelina, then, at the sight of her stepmother's stony look, fell silent. Mrs. Winston did not *want* to believe her and therefore *would not* believe her.

"Where is the Duke now?" asked Mrs. Winston.

"He – had an accident. He fell. Someone went to his aid."

"Well! I'd better send the footman for a doctor and you'd better retire to your room. I'm sure the Duke is most upset that you abandoned him."

Abandoned him! thought Madelina bitterly, as Mrs. Winston rushed out to summon the footman.

She listened at the half-open door for a moment, then slipped out and ran up to her room. There she found Beth in her nightgown and cap with a lamp in her hand.

"Oh, miss, what's goin' on? I heard the bell."

Madelina told Beth all with an air of desperation.

After what had happened this evening, she could not countenance marrying the Duke.

What should she do?

Beth thought a moment and then brightened.

"Go to Lady Bamber in London, miss. This very instant. Don't waste time or your stepmother will probably lock you in your room till the Weddin' day."

"Perhaps the Duke won't want to marry me now," ventured Madelina hopefully.

"No such luck," said Beth grimly. "He'll want you even more, knowin' his sort."

Beth threw some clothes into a carpet bag. They had little money between them, but enough, Beth thought, for a coach fare to London.

Then they heard a commotion in the hall below that suggested the Duke, and whoever had come to his aid, had arrived back at the house.

Beth advised Madelina to take the backstairs and leave the house through the kitchen.

It was gone eleven as Madelina set forth in her long woollen cloak.

The turn of events had all happened so swiftly that even as she hurried along the silent streets she could not quite digest her situation.

She had to get out of the town, for the Duke would surely send someone after her.

Hearing the sound of wheels ahead, she shrank in against a dark wall as a carriage hurtled past, the horses straining at their reins. Madelina caught just a glimpse of a figure leaning out at the window urging the coachman on.

There was no time to wonder who this impatient traveller might be. She decided to turn away from the sea as she was sure that she had spotted a hostelry on the edge of town and it was likely that an early coach would set off from there to London.

The air seemed to be growing colder by the minute as she hurried on. A harsh night breeze blew up and then suddenly the Heavens opened and rain fell furiously.

Within a short time she was soaked, but she drove herself on. She had to get away, *away*!

As her mother had taught her, she started to pray, as she had never prayed before, that God would save her from the terrible Fate that must surely befall her.

A Church bell tolled midnight. She had been on the road for half an hour at least and had not yet come upon the hostelry, so she prayed even more fervently from the very depths of her soul.

Hearing again the sound of wheels, this time from behind her, she glanced over her shoulder and then saw a carriage fast approaching.

Had the Duke discovered her absence so soon?

She drew up the hood of her cloak and began to run, hoping to see a lane or alleyway to turn into.

She heard someone leap from the carriage while it was still moving and footsteps pursue her.

Someone called her name, she stumbled and an arm closed tightly about her body. She would have screamed out, but a hand was clasped over her mouth and she was dragged struggling towards the carriage.

She was lifted in and half thrown onto a seat.

Her assailant then slammed the door shut and called out to the coachman to drive on.

Madelina hid her face in her hands as the carriage started up.

She was caught!

Her Fate was finally sealed!

"Madelina!"

The voice that softly called her name was familiar, but it was not the Duke's. She hardly dared breathe as she slowly took her hands from her face and looked up.

"Oliver!"

De Burge leaned forward and gently pushed down the hood of her cloak.

"Darling!"

"No – no – not that! You cannot call me that!" Madelina cried out in horror.

De Burge ran his eyes over her and seemed to make a decision to wait until she was calmer before attempting conversation.

"Take off that wet cloak," he commanded.

Madelina, a memory of the Duke's tone of voice ringing in her ears, was filled with sudden fear.

"My c-cloak? Why? What do you want?"

De Burge's brow furrowed to see her so distressed.

"What happened? Why did you flee?"

Madelina gazed at him suspiciously.

"How do you know I fled? Who have you spoken to? Where – " and her eyes rushed to the window. "Where are we going? Not back? *Never* back?"

"Hush, hush, Madelina." De Burge leaned forward, and gently pushed the wet strands of hair from her face.

"We are not going back. I am now taking you to London to Lady Bamber. She told me you had been kidnapped, more or less, and brought here. I raced down to find you. Your stepmother refused to speak to me and slammed the door in my face."

Here he caught his breath and then continued,

"But Beth crept out and told me that you had run away, although neither your stepmother nor the Duke had yet found out. She heard Mrs. Winston calling her then and had to return to the house, so I have no idea why – "

He stopped as he saw Madelina begin to shake.

"Please take off your cloak," he said. "It's so wet. Have mine. Here wrap it around you. Now tell me what happened to you back there?"

"The Duke – ," Madelina faltered. "We were out for a stroll and he suggested – we go to the beach. On the path he – took me by the waist – and touched me here – "

Madelina's hand moved to her breast and she shook even more as she relived the moment.

De Burge's eyes blazed. His fist curled at his side and he brought it down so hard on the door of the carriage that Madelina gave a cry, fearing that he had hurt himself.

He then reassured her,

"It's all right, Madelina. My beloved, it's all right."

Madelina's eyes widened in alarm.

"You called me – 'beloved'. You must not, Oliver. For my sake, you must not."

His features softened as he gazed at her and then on an impulse, he slid to his knees before her and caught her hands in his. He pressed them to his chest.

She stared at him, scared at her longing to yield and then he said,

"Listen, Madelina. There is nothing to prevent us being to each other what we once were. *Nothing*!"

"Nothing!" she echoed, now really mystified.

He hesitated, released her hands and rose from his knees to seat himself opposite her again.

"If you had only been able to stay on at that play," he said quietly and slowly, "you would have been spared this disagreeable incident with the Duke."

"The play?"

De Burge gave a wry laugh.

"The play was the thing, Madelina. Oswald Vane did indeed take it upon himself to give the full story. But it was not the story we had been told."

Madelina sat up expectantly.

She felt a strange lightening of her heart, as if hope had entered there, like a little songbird.

De Burge had not known what to do when she was hurried away by the Duke, who was her fiancé, after all.

He had sat on in the box, deeply disturbed by what he had just witnessed and it was only gradually that his attention was drawn to what was happening on the stage.

The characters in the play were 'Mr. Wilton', based as Madelina knew on Mr. Winston – and a woman called 'Angelina', based on Adelaide Anderson, who then became Mrs. de Burge.

Wilton had fallen in love with Angelina and hoped to marry her. She encouraged his attentions, enjoying the gifts he lavishly showered on her, but would not accept his proposal. Unbeknownst to her young admirer, she was all the time embroiled in an affair with a rich man who called himself 'Sturrocks', who she suspected to be an aristocrat.

When Sturrocks then discovered that Angelina was expecting his child, he disappeared. Since Sturrocks was an assumed name, she could not trace him.

In despair she turned to Wilton, who then agreed to marry her and give the child his own name. Angelina was grateful until Wilton's appalled parents disowned him.

Wilton now had no inheritance and as such ceased to be an attractive proposition.

Within only a few days Angelina eloped with yet another suitor, called in the play 'Burgess', but obviously based on the elder Mr. de Burge.

The heartbroken and penniless Mr. Wilton booked a passage to America –

"So you see, Madelina," finished de Burge, "you and I are not related after all. My father is the mysterious Sturrocks, or rather, the man he was based on. I can call you darling, beloved, sweetheart and there is no one in the whole world who can stop me."

Madelina let out a cry and tears spilled from her eyes.

"We are *not* – brother and sister?"

"No."

"Then why – did your mother say – that we were?"

De Burge looked grim.

"My mother and I have long not seen eye to eye on the question of who I might marry. It's one of the reasons we are somewhat estranged. She was obsessed with my marrying into the aristocracy and so she was delighted with the idea of an alliance with Earl Villers. When Lady Kitty wrote to inform her of the attraction evolving between you and me, my mother took action. She concocted a wild story that would mean we must part forever."

"How wicked of her!" exclaimed Madelina. "And to slander my poor father so!"

"Yes. That my own mother should have done such a thing fills me with despair. I have cut off all relations with her and my stepfather is, I am glad to say, on my side for once."

He leaned forward and put a hand on Madelina's knee.

"Don't you realise, Madelina? We are now free to marry. After all this with the Duke, you owe him nothing."

Madelina's features lit up for an instant only.

Then her face fell.

"But Oliver," she whispered, "you – you are not free. There is still Lady Kitty."

De Burge sat back with an angry frown.

"Lady Kitty! I believe that she colluded with my mother in this story, though neither admits it, and I cannot prove it."

"If you cannot prove it," said Madelina miserably, "then how can you withdraw from the – *marriage*?"

The word acted on her spirits like a stopper drawn from a bottle and she burst into heartrending sobs.

De Burge moved to her side, pulling a handkerchief from his pocket.

"T-that!" she stammered between sobs, seeing the familiar kerchief that she had once bound his hand with.

"That," he repeated with a smile, dabbing her eyes, and then bringing it to his lips with an ardour that took her breath away. "I have kissed this so often since learning the truth of my parentage, for it was all I had of you in my possession. But now you are here and I may take you in my arms with no compunction and no fear!"

"But – but Lady Kitty!" Madelina persisted.

De Burge gave a smile.

"Ah. Lady Kitty. Well, let me tell you. After the play, which I left with a feeling of great joy, I went to see Oswald Vane. I then asked him who my real father – the 'Sturrocks' character in the play – might be. He did not know for sure, but he had often heard a certain gentleman in a London Club bemoaning his lack of a legitimate male heir.

"'Begad,' he would say, 'I have an illegitimate one somewhere, I am sure, and if I could find him I would most certainly acknowledge him. His mother was a common dancer, although beautiful enough. I think she married and went away, for I have never seen her in Society'.

"I asked Vane who this gentleman was and do you know what he answered?"

Madelina, mesmerised, shook her head.

"Earl Villers!" said Oliver with an air of jubilation, enjoying Madelina's astonished response. "Oh, my darling, do you see where my story is heading? I went to the Earl and I asked him if the name of that 'common dancer' who had borne his child was Adelaide. When he replied that it was, I announced that in that case, I was his son.

Madelina looked even more incredulous.

"He wanted to make me his heir there and then. Because my mother had moved North when she married de Burge – because she had never gone into Society – he had never seen her again. And she had never known that the lover she knew as Sturrocks was in fact heir to the wealthy Villers estate."

Madelina gazed speechlessly at de Burge, her eyes wide and glistening.

"So you do see, Madelina, I can never marry Lady Kitty. For she is in effect my half-sister. Although a half-sister who must resent my existence, since I have more or less disinherited her! But I am free. Free to call you my darling, beloved, whatever I will, and now *my wife!*"

De Burge leaned down his head and Madelina lifted her face and their lips met in a kiss that felt like a shower of sparks enveloping them.

How long it lasted she could not tell, but she knew that it was a sacred seal of love. The very blood in her veins raced to mingle with his.

She was touching the stars, she was flying to the moon and dancing on the Milky Way.

Never had she dreamed that she could feel like this.

When at last they broke apart, his eyes were dark with passion, his face set with determination.

"You know what I intend to do with you now?" he asked huskily.

"N-no."

"I am taking you straight to Lady Bamber's house, where she is organising a Wedding. And I shall marry you tomorrow. And it cannot come too soon, for I long with my whole being to love you. It is all I can do to stay my hands here in this carriage, but I must or you will think me no better than the Duke!"

"Never!"

As if to reassure him, she sought his lips again. Her heart leapt as she felt his hands encircle her waist and then heard him groan.

The carriage was racing towards their marriage and her thoughts raced with it.

Soon she would be in a linen nightgown, her hair flowing about her shoulders, as she crossed the floor to her husband's arms.

She had crossed an ocean – an ocean of love – to find the one man in the world who could make her heart beat so gloriously and her pulse race so fiercely that she thought she would die.

Oliver's thoughts seemed to be moving in the same passionate direction, for he next undid the ribbon that tied up her hair and held the loosened locks in his fist.

"How I long to watch you coming to me, coming to my heart," he murmured, his breath close to her cheek. "I ache to hold you in my arms. Do forgive me, Madelina, but I am only a man, a man who has struggled so hard with his desire since he first set eyes on you."

Drawing his head to her breast, she whispered her forgiveness.

It was not long now before she would be his for ever and ever.

Her prayers had all been answered and God had blessed them both.

And He had given them, against what had seemed insuperable odds, a happiness that could only be Divine.

They would love each other for Eternity however many lives it took and there would very many.

Love had brought them together, Love would guide them throughout the years ahead and Love would cover and protect their souls.

10091260R00089

Printed in Great Britain
by Amazon